PUFFIN BOOKS

THICK AS THIEVES

Born in Kasauli (Himachal Pradesh) in 1934, Ruskin Bond grew up in Jamnagar (Gujarat), Dehradun, New Delhi and Shimla.

His first novel *The Room on the Roof*, written when he was seventeen, received the John Llewellyn Rhys Memorial Prize in 1957. Since then he has written over five hundred short stories, essays and novellas (some included in the collections *Dust on the Mountains* and *Classic Ruskin Bond*) and more than forty books for children. He received the Sahitya Akademi Award for English writing in India in 1993, the Padma Shri in 1999, and the Delhi government's Lifetime Achievement Award in 2012. He was recently awarded the Sahitya Akademi's Bal Sahitya Puraskar for his 'total contribution to children's literature'. He lives in Landour, Mussoorie, with his extended family.

Also in Puffin by Ruskin Bond

Thick as Thieves

Tales of Friendship

RUSKIN BOND

PUFFIN BOOKS

PUFFIN BOOKS

USA | Canada | UK | Ireland | Australia
New Zealand | India | South Africa | China

Puffin Books is part of the Penguin Random House group of
companies whose addresses can be found at global.penguinrandomhouse.com

Published by Penguin Random House India Pvt. Ltd
7th Floor, Infinity Tower C, DLF Cyber City,
Gurgaon 122 002, Haryana, India

Penguin
Random House
India

First published in Puffin by Penguin Books India 2013

Copyright © Ruskin Bond 2013

10 9 8 7 6 5 4 3 2

ISBN 9780143332480

Typeset in Minion Pro by Eleven Arts, Delhi
Printed at Repro India Ltd, Navi Mumbai

www.penguinbooksindia.com

'Make friends, make friends, however strong
Or weak they may be:
Recall the captive elephants
That the mice set free.'

—*The Panchatantra* [Book 2]

Contents

Contents

Introduction

'One good father is more than a hundred schoolmasters,' wrote George Herbert, and I was very fortunate in having a father who had, in fact, been a schoolmaster before joining the Royal Air Force at the outbreak of World War II. When I was a little boy he took me by the hand and led me up the steps of old forts and monuments, and told me their stories. Through books and pictures and postage stamps, he gave me a solid grounding in history and geography. He was the best friend a small boy could have had. I lost him when I was only ten, but in spirit he continued to walk beside me through the passing years. For to live in the hearts of those we leave behind is never to die.

After his passing I was stranded for a while. It took me a few years to adjust to the very different lifestyles of my mother and stepfather. For some time, books were my best friends. And then, as I settled down in boarding school and showed that I could kick a football as well as write an essay, I found that friends came to me without much effort on my part. The 'four feathers' were real enough, and so was Omar (name changed) and others whom I have yet to write about. In the year after I finished school there were Somi and Ranbir and Co. After leaving India I spent two or three lonely years in Jersey and

London; the letters from these friends helped to sustain me. Then, in London, I met some Vietnamese students and young West Indians, who brightened my days in that lonely city.

Returning to India, I found myself part of Kamal's family in Delhi and then Prem's family in Mussoorie. From individual friends I had progressed to entire families!

I think those lonely periods, in my childhood and then abroad, had made me value friendships more than most people do.

'Friendship is a sheltering tree,' wrote Coleridge. True, a good friend is like a tree—steadfast, sturdy, comforting, ever-present: until we cut it down. So we must preserve our friendships as we preserve our protective trees.

But—'Beware of false friends,' warns the Hitopadesa. So we must choose our friends wisely and in accordance with our own natures. It can take a long time to know anyone really well.

Ruskin Bond

The Four Feathers

Our school dormitory was a very long room with about thirty beds, fifteen on either side of the room. This was good for pillow fights. Class V would take on Class IV (the two senior classes in our prep school) and there would be plenty of space for leaping, struggling small boys, pillows flying, feathers flying, until there was a cry of 'Here comes Fishy!' or 'Here comes Olly!' and either Mr Fisher, the headmaster, or Mr Oliver, the Senior Master, would come striding in, cane in hand, to put an end to the general mayhem. Pillow fights were allowed, up to a point; nobody got hurt. But parents sometimes complained, if at the end of the term, a boy came home with a pillow devoid of cotton wool or feathers.

In that last year at prep school in Shimla, there were four of us who were close friends—Bimal, whose home was in Bombay; Riaz, who came from Lahore, Bran, who hailed from Vellore; and your narrator, who lived wherever his father (then in the Air Force) was posted.

We called ourselves the 'Four Feathers', the feathers signifying that we were companions in adventure, comrades-in-arms, and knights of the round table. Bimal adopted a peacock's feather as his emblem—he was always a bit showy. Riaz chose a falcon's feather—although we couldn't find one. Bran and I were at first offered crow or hen feathers, but we protested vigorously and threatened a walkout, finally I settled for a parrot's feather (taken from Mrs Fisher's pet parrot), and Bran found a woodpecker's, which suited him, as he was always knocking things about.

Bimal was all thin legs and arms, so light and frisky that at times he seemed to be walking on air. We called him 'Bambi', after the delicate little deer in the Disney film. Riaz, on the other hand, was a sturdy boy, good at games though not very studious; but always good-natured and smiling.

Bran was a dark, good-looking boy from the South; he was just a little spoilt—hated being given out in a cricket match and would refuse to leave the crease! But he was affectionate and a loyal friend. I was the 'scribe'—good at inventing stories in order to get out of scrapes—but hopeless at sums, my highest marks being 22 out of 100.

On Sunday afternoons, when there were no classes or organized games, we were allowed to roam about on the hillside below the school. The four feathers would laze about on the short summer grass, sharing the occasional food parcel from home, reading comics (sometimes a book) and making plans for the long winter holidays. My father, who collected everything from stamps to seashells to butterflies, had given me a butterfly net and urged me to try and catch a rare species which, he said, was found only near Chotta Shimla. He described it as a large, purple butterfly with yellow and black borders on its wings. A 'Purple Emperor', I think it was called. As I wasn't very good at identifying butterflies, I would chase anything that happened to flit across the school grounds, usually ending up with common 'Red Admirals', 'Clouded Yellows', or 'Cabbage Whites'. But that

Purple Emperor—that rare specimen being sought by collectors the world over—proved elusive. I would have to seek my fortune in some other line of endeavour.

One day, scrambling about among the rocks and thorny bushes below the school, I almost fell over a small bundle lying in the shade of a young spruce tree. On taking a closer look, I discovered that the bundle was really a baby, wrapped up in a tattered, old blanket.

'Feathers, feathers!' I called, 'come here and look. A baby's been left here!'

The feathers joined me and we all stared down at the infant, who was fast asleep.

'Who would leave a baby on the hillside?' asked Bimal to no one in particular.

'Someone who doesn't want it,' said Bran.

'And hoped some good people would come along and keep it,' added Riaz.

'A panther might have come along instead,' I declared. 'Can't leave it here.'

'Well, we'll just have to adopt it,' said Bimal.

'We can't adopt a baby,' protested Bran.

'Why not?'

'We have to be married.'

'We don't.'

'Not us, you dope. The grown-ups who adopt babies.'

'Well, we can't just leave it here for grown-ups to come along,' I said.

'We don't even know if it's a boy or a girl,' said Riaz.'

'Makes no difference. A baby's a baby. Let's take it back to school.'

'And keep it in the dormitory?'

'Of course not. Who's going to feed it? Babies need milk. We'll hand it over to Mrs Fisher. She doesn't have a baby.'

'Maybe she doesn't want one. Look, it's beginning to cry. Let's hurry!'

Riaz picked up the wide awake and crying baby and gave it to Bimal who gave it to Bran who gave it to me. The four feathers marched up the hill to school with a very noisy baby.

'Now it's done potty in the blanket,' I complained, 'and some of it's on my shirt.'

'Never mind,' said Bimal. 'It's for a good cause. You're a Boy Scout, remember? You're supposed to help people in distress.'

The headmaster and his wife were in their drawing room, enjoying their afternoon tea and cakes. We trudged in, and Bimal announced, 'We've got something for Mrs Fisher.'

Mrs Fisher took one look at the bundle in my arms and let out a shriek. 'What have you brought here, Bond?'

'A baby, ma'am. I think it's a girl. Do you want to adopt it?'

Mrs Fisher threw up her hands in consternation, and turned to her husband. 'What are we to do, Frank? These boys are impossible. They've picked up someone's child!'

'We'll have to inform the police,' declared Mr Fisher, reaching for the telephone. 'We can't have lost babies in the school.'

Just then there was a commotion outside, and a wild-eyed woman, her clothes dishevelled, entered through the front door accompanied by several menfolk from one of the nearby villages. She ran towards us, crying out, 'My baby, my baby! *Mera bachcha*! You've stolen my baby!'

'We found it on the hillside,' I stammered.

'That's right,' said Bran. 'Finders keepers!'

'Quiet, Adams,' scolded Mr Fisher, holding up his hand for order and addressing the villagers in a friendly manner. 'These boys found the baby alone on the hillside and brought it here before . . . before . . .'

'Before the hyenas got it,' I put in.

'Quite right, Bond. And why did you leave your child alone?' he asked the woman.

'I put her down for five minutes so that I could climb the plum tree and collect the plums. When I came down, the baby had gone! But I could hear it crying up on the hill. I called the menfolk and we come looking for it.'

'Well, here's your baby,' I said, thrusting it into her arms. By then I was glad to rid of it! 'Look after it properly in the future.'

'Kidnapper!' she screamed at me.

Mr Fisher succeeded in mollifying the villagers. 'These boys are good Scouts,' he told them. 'It's their business to help people.'

'Scout Law Number Three, sir,' I added. 'To be useful and helpful.'

And then the headmaster turned the tables on the villagers. 'By the way, those plum trees belong to the school. So do the peaches and apricots. Now I know why they've been disappearing so fast!'

The villagers, a little chastened, went their way. Mr Fisher reached for his cane. From the way he fondled it I knew he was itching to use it on our bottoms.

'No, Frank,' said Mrs Fisher, intervening on our behalf, 'It was really very sweet of them to look after that baby. And look at Bond—he's got baby-poo all over his clothes.'

'So he has. Go and take a bath, all of you. And what are you grinning about, Bond?'

'Scout Law Number Eight, sir. A Scout smiles and whistles under all difficulties.'

And so ended the first adventure of the four feathers.

Best Favourite Friend

[Somi was Rusty's first Indian friend when he ran away from his guardian's home and struck out on his own. The Kapoor family, who took him in, have broken up after the death of their friend Kishen's mother. In this chapter from *The Room on the Roof*, Somi and Rusty ponder upon an uncertain future . . .]

It was a sticky, restless afternoon. The water-carrier passed below the room with his skin bag, spraying water on the dusty path. The toy seller entered the compound, calling his wares in a high-pitched sing-song voice, and presently there was the chatter of children.

The toy seller had a long bamboo pole, crossed by two or three shorter bamboos, from which hung all manner of toys—little celluloid drums, tin watches, tiny flutes and whistles, and multicoloured rag dolls—and when these ran out, they were replaced by others from a large bag, a most mysterious and fascinating bag, one into which no one but the toy seller was allowed to look. He was a popular person with the rich and poor alike, for his toys never cost more than four annas and never lasted longer than a day.

Rusty liked the cheap toys, and was fond of decorating his room with them. He bought a two-anna flute and walked upstairs, blowing on it.

He removed his shirt and sandals and lay flat on the bed staring up at the ceiling. The lizards scuttled along the rafters, the bald mynah hopped along the window ledge. He was about to fall asleep when Somi came into the room.

Somi looked listless.

'I feel sticky,' he said, 'I don't want to wear any clothes.'

Somi pulled off his shirt and deposited it on the table, then stood before the mirror, studying his physique. Then he turned to Rusty.

'You don't look well,' he said, 'there are cobwebs in your hair.'

'I don't care.'

'You must have been very fond of Mrs Kapoor. She was very kind.'

'I loved her, didn't you know?'

'No. My own love is the only thing I know. Rusty, best favourite friend, you cannot stay here in this room, you must come back to my house. Besides, this building will soon have new tenants.'

'I'll get out when they come, or when the landlord discovers I'm still living here.'

Somi's usually bright face was somewhat morose, and there was a faint agitation showing in his eyes.

'I will go and get a cucumber to eat,' he said. 'Then there is something to tell you.'

'I don't want a cucumber,' protested Rusty, 'I want a coconut.'

'I want a cucumber.'

Rusty felt irritable. The room was hot, the bed was hot, his blood was hot. Impatiently, he said, 'Go and eat your cucumber, I don't want any . . .'

Somi looked at him with pained surprise; then, without a word, picked up his shirt and marched out of the room. Rusty could hear the slap of his slippers on the stairs, and then the bicycle tyres on the gravel path.

'Hey, Somi!' shouted Rusty, leaping off the bed and running out on to the roof. 'Come back!'

But the bicycle jumped over the ditch, and Somi's shirt flapped, and there was nothing Rusty could do but return to bed. He was alarmed at his liverish ill temper. He lay down again and stared at the ceiling, at the lizards chasing each other across the rafters. On the roof two crows were fighting, knocking each other's feathers out. Everyone was in a temper.

What's wrong? wondered Rusty. I spoke to Somi in fever, not in anger, but my words were angry. Now I am miserable, fed up. Oh, hell . . .

He closed his eyes and shut out everything.

He opened his eyes to laughter. Somi's face was close, laughing into Rusty's.

'Of what were you dreaming, Rusty, I have never seen you smile so sweetly!'

'Oh, I wasn't dreaming,' answered Rusty, sitting up and feeling better now that Somi had returned. 'I am sorry for being so grumpy, but I'm not feeling . . .'

'Quiet!' admonished Somi, putting a finger to the other's lips. 'See, I have settled the matter. Here is a coconut for you, and here is a cucumber for me!'

They sat cross-legged on the bed, facing each other, Somi with his cucumber, and Rusty with his coconut. The coconut milk trickled down Rusty's chin and on to his chest, giving him a cool, pleasant sensation.

Rusty said, 'I am afraid for Kishen. I am sure he will give trouble to his relatives, and they are not like his parents. Mr Kapoor will have no say without Meena.'

Somi was silent. The only sound was the munching of the cucumber and the coconut. He looked at Rusty, an uncertain smile on his lips but none in his eyes, and, in a forced conversational manner, said, 'I'm going to Amritsar for a few months. But I will be back in the spring. Rusty, you will be all right here . . .'

This news was so unexpected that for some time Rusty could not take it in. The thought had never occurred to him that one day Somi too might leave Dehra, just as Ranbir and Suri and Kishen had done. Rusty could not speak. A sickening heaviness clogged his heart and brain.

'Hey, Rusty!' laughed Somi. 'Don't look as though there is poison in the coconut!'

The poison lay in Somi's words. And the poison worked, running through Rusty's veins and beating against his heart and hammering on his brain. The poison worked, wounding him.

He began, 'Somi . . .' but could go no further.

'Finish the coconut!'

'Somi,' said Rusty again, 'if you are leaving Dehra, Somi, then I am leaving too.'

'Eat the coco . . . what did you say?'

'I am going too.'

'Are you mad?'

'Not at all.'

Serious now, and troubled, Somi put his hand on his friend's wrist. He shook his head; he could not understand.

'Why, Rusty? Where?'

'England.'

'But you haven't any money, you silly fool!'

'I can get an assisted passage. The British government will pay.'

'You are a British subject?'

'I don't know . . .'

'*Toba!*' Somi slapped his thighs and looked upwards in despair. 'You are neither an Indian subject nor a British subject, and you think someone is going to pay for your passage! And how are you to get a passport?'

'How?' asked Rusty, anxious to find out.

'*Toba!* Have you a birth certificate?'

'Oh, no.'

'Then you are not born,' decreed Somi, with a certain amount of satisfaction. 'You are not alive! You do not happen to be in this world!'

He paused for breath, then waved his finger in the air. 'Rusty, you cannot go!' he said.

Rusty lay down despondently.

'I never really thought I would,' he said. 'I only said I would because I felt like it. Not because I am unhappy—I have never been happier elsewhere—but because I am restless as I have always been. I don't suppose I'll be anywhere for long . . .'

He spoke the truth. Rusty always spoke the truth. He defined truth as a feeling, and when he said what he felt, he said the truth. (Only he didn't always speak his feelings.) He never lied. You don't have to lie if you know how to withhold the truth.

'You belong here,' continued Somi, trying to reconcile Rusty with circumstance. 'You will get lost in big cities. Rusty, you will break your heart. And when you come back—if you come back—I will be grown-up and you will be grown-up—I mean more than we are now—and we will be like strangers to each other . . . And besides, there are no chaat shops in England!'

'But I don't belong here, Somi. I don't belong anywhere. Even if I have papers, I don't belong. I'm a half-caste, I know it, and that is as good as not belonging anywhere.'

What am I saying, thought Rusty, why do I make my inheritance a justification for my present bitterness? No one has cast me out . . . of my own free will I want to run away from India . . . why do I blame inheritance?

'It can also mean that you belong everywhere,' said Somi. 'But you never told me. You are fair like a European.'

'I had not thought much about it.'

'Are you ashamed?'

'No. My guardian was. He kept it to himself, he only told

12

me when I came home after playing Holi. I was happy then. So, when he told me, I was not ashamed, I was proud.'

'And now?'

'Now? Oh, I can't really believe it. Somehow I do not really feel mixed.'

'Then don't blame it for nothing.'

Rusty felt a little ashamed, and they were both silent awhile, then Somi shrugged and said, 'So you are going. You are running away from India.'

'No, not from India.'

'Then you are running away from your friends, from me!'

Rusty felt the irony of this remark, and allowed a tone of sarcasm into his voice.

'*You*, Master Somi, *you* are the one who is going away. I am still here. *You* are going to Amritsar. I only *want* to go. And I'm here alone; everyone has gone. So if I do eventually leave, the only person I'll be running away from will be myself.'

'Ah!' said Somi, nodding his head wisely. 'And by running away from yourself, you will be running away from me and India! Now come on, let's go and have chaat.'

He pulled Rusty off the bed, and pushed him out of the room. Then, at the top of the steps, he leapt lightly on Rusty's back, kicked him with his heels, and shouted: 'Down the steps, my *tuttoo*, my pony! Fast down the steps!'

So Rusty carried him downstairs and dropped him on the grass. They laughed: but there was no great joy in their laughter, they laughed for the sake of friendship.

Ruskin Bond

'Best favourite friend,' said Somi, throwing a handful of mud in Rusty's face.

Author's Note: From *The Room on the Roof*, my first novel. The character of Somi was taken straight from the journal I kept when I was sixteen. Over sixty years later, we are still in touch. Somi lives in America with his sons and their families, and I am back in India.

Rusty Plays Holi

[From *The Room on the Roof*]

In the early morning, when it was still dark, Ranbir stopped in the jungle behind Mr Harrison's house, and slapped his drum. His thick mass of hair was covered with red dust and his body, naked but for a cloth round his waist, was smeared with green; he looked like a painted god, a green god. After a minute he slapped the drum again, then sat down on his heels and waited.

Rusty woke to the sound of the second drumbeat, and lay in bed and listened; it was repeated, travelling over the still air and in through the bedroom window. *Dhum!* . . . A double beat now, one deep, one high, insistent, questioning . . . Rusty remembered his promise, that he would play Holi with Ranbir, meet him in the jungle when he beat the drum. But he had made the promise on the condition that his guardian did not return; he could not possibly keep it now, not after the thrashing he had received.

Dhum-dhum, spoke the drum in the forest; *dhum-dhum*, impatient and getting annoyed . . .

'Why can't he shut up,' muttered Rusty, 'does he want to wake Mr Harrison . . .'

Holi, the festival of colours, the arrival of spring, the rebirth of the new year, the awakening of love, what were these things to him. They did not concern his life, he could not start a new life, not for one day . . . and besides, it all sounded very primitive, this splashing of colour and beating of drums . . .

Dhum-dhum!

The boy sat up in bed.

The sky had grown lighter.

From the distant bazaar came a new music, many drums and voices, faint but steady, growing in rhythm and excitement. The sound conveyed something to Rusty, something wild and emotional, something that belonged to his dreamworld, and on a sudden impulse he sprang out of bed.

He went to the door and listened, the house was quiet, he bolted the door. The colours of Holi, he knew, would stain his clothes, so he did not remove his pyjamas. In an old pair of flattened rubber-soled tennis shoes, he climbed out of the window and ran over the dew-wet grass, down the path behind the house, over the hill and into the jungle.

When Ranbir saw the boy approach, he rose from the ground. The long hand drum, the dholak, hung at his waist. As he rose, the sun rose. But the sun did not look as fiery as Ranbir who, in Rusty's eyes, appeared as a painted demon, rather than a god.

'You are late, mister,' said Ranbir. 'I thought you were not coming.'

He had both fists closed, but when he walked towards Rusty

he opened them, smiling widely, a white smile on a green face. In his right hand was the red dust and in his left hand the green dust. And with his right hand he rubbed the red dust on Rusty's left cheek, and then with the other hand he put the green dust on the boy's right cheek; then he stood back and looked at Rusty and laughed. Then, according to the custom, he embraced the bewildered boy. It was a wrestler's hug, and Rusty winced breathlessly.

'Come,' said Ranbir, 'let us go and make the town a rainbow.'

~

And truly, that day there was an outbreak of spring.

The sun came up, and the bazaar woke up. The walls of the houses were suddenly patched with splashes of colour, and just as suddenly the trees seemed to have burst into flower, for in the forest there were armies of rhododendrons, and by the river the poinsettias danced; the cherry and the plum were in blossom; the snow in the mountains had melted, and the streams were rushing torrents; the new leaves on the trees were full of sweetness, the young grass held both dew and sun, and made an emerald of every dewdrop.

The infection of spring spread simultaneously through the world of man and the world of nature, and made them one.

Ranbir and Rusty moved round the hill, keeping near the fringes of the jungle until they had skirted not only the European community but also the smart shopping centre. They came down dirty little side streets where the walls of houses, stained with the wear and tear of many years of meagre habitation, were now stained again with the vivid colours of Holi. They came to the Clock Tower.

At the Tower, spring had already been declared open. Clouds of coloured dust rose in the air and spread, and jets of water—green and orange and purple, all rich, emotional colours—burst out everywhere.

Children formed groups. They were armed mainly with bicycle pumps, or pumps fashioned from bamboo stems, from which squirted liquid colour. The children paraded the main road, chanting shrilly and clapping their hands. The men and women preferred the dust to the water. They too sang, but their chanting held a significance, their hands and fingers drummed the rhythms of spring, the same rhythms, the same songs that belonged to this day every year of their lives.

Ranbir was met by some friends and greeted with great hilarity. A bicycle pump was directed at Rusty and a jet of sooty black water squirted into his face.

Blinded for a moment, Rusty blundered about in great confusion. A horde of children bore down on him, and he was subjected to a pumping from all sides. His shirt and pyjamas, drenched through, stuck to his skin; then someone gripped the end of his shirt and tugged at it until it tore and came away. Dust was thrown on the boy, on his face and body, roughly and with full force, and his tender, underexposed skin smarted beneath the onslaught.

Then his eyes cleared. He blinked and looked wildly around at the group of boys and girls who cheered and danced in front of him. His body was running mostly with sooty black, streaked with red, and his mouth seemed full of it too, and he began to spit.

Then, one by one, Ranbir's friends approached Rusty.

Gently, they rubbed dust on the boy's cheeks, and embraced him; they were like so many flaming demons that Rusty could not distinguish one from the other. But this gentle greeting, coming so soon after the stormy bicycle pump attack, bewildered Rusty even more.

Ranbir said, 'Now you are one of us, come.' And Rusty went with him and the others.

'Suri is hiding,' cried someone. 'He has locked himself in his house and won't play Holi!'

'Well, he will have to play,' said Ranbir, 'even if we break the house down.'

Suri, who dreaded Holi, had decided to spend the day in a state of siege; he had set up camp in his mother's kitchen, where there were provisions enough for the whole day. He listened to his playmates calling to him from the courtyard, and ignored their invitations, jeers, and threats; the door was strong and well barricaded.

But the youths outside, intoxicated by the drumming and shouting and high spirits, were not going to be done out of the pleasure of discomfiting Suri. So they acquired a ladder and made their entry into the kitchen by the skylight.

Suri squealed with fright. The door was opened and he was bundled out, and his spectacles were trampled.

'My glasses!' he screamed. 'You've broken them!'

'You can afford a dozen pairs!' jeered one of his antagonists.

'But I can't see, you fools, I can't see!'

'He can't see!' cried someone in scorn. 'For once in his life, Suri can't see what's going on! Now, whenever he spies, we'll smash his glasses!'

Not knowing Suri very well, Rusty could not help pitying the frantic boy.

'Why don't you let him go,' he asked Ranbir. 'Don't force him if he doesn't want to play.'

'But this is the only chance we have of repaying him for all his dirty tricks. It is the only day on which no one is afraid of him!'

Rusty could not imagine how anyone could possibly be afraid of the pale, struggling, spindly-legged boy who was almost being torn apart, and was glad when the others had finished their sport with him.

All day Rusty roamed the town and countryside with Ranbir and his friends, and Suri was soon forgotten. For one day, Ranbir and his friends forgot their homes and their work and the problem of the next meal, and danced down the roads, out of town and into the forest. And, for one day, Rusty forgot his guardian and the missionary's wife and the supple Malacca cane, and ran with the others through the town and into the forest.

The crisp, sunny morning ripened into afternoon.

In the forest, in the cool dark silence of the jungle, they stopped singing and shouting, suddenly exhausted. They lay down in the shade of many trees, and the grass was soft and comfortable, and very soon everyone except Rusty was fast asleep.

Rusty was tired. He was hungry. He had lost his shirt and shoes, his feet were bruised, his body sore. It was only now, resting, that he noticed these things, for he had been caught up in the excitement of the colour game, overcome by an exhilaration he had never known. His fair hair was tousled and streaked with colour, and his eyes were wide with wonder.

He was exhausted now, but he was happy.

He wanted this to go on forever, this day of feverish emotion, this life in another world. He did not want to leave the forest; it was safe; its earth soothed him, gathered him in so that the pain of his body became a pleasure . . .

He did not want to go home.

Reunion at the Regal

If you want to see a ghost, just stand outside New Delhi's Regal Cinema for twenty minutes or so. The approach to the grand old cinema hall is a great place for them. Sooner or later you'll see a familiar face in the crowd. Before you have time to recall who it was or who it may be, the face will have disappeared and you will be left wondering if it really was so-and-so . . . because surely so-and-so died several years ago . . .

The Regal was very posh in the early 1940s when, in the company of my father, I watched my first film there. The Connaught Place cinemas still had a new look about them, and they played the latest offerings from Hollywood and Britain. To see a Hindi film, you had to travel all the way to Kashmere Gate or Chandni Chowk.

Over the years, I was in and out of the Regal quite a few times, and so I became used to meeting old acquaintances or glimpsing familiar faces in the foyer or on the steps outside.

On one occasion I was mistaken for a ghost.

I was about thirty at the time. I was standing on the steps of the arcade, waiting for someone, when a young Indian man came up to me and said something in German or what sounded like German.

'I'm sorry,' I said. 'I don't understand. You may speak to me in English or Hindi.'

'Aren't you Hans? We met in Frankfurt last year.'

'I'm sorry, I've never been to Frankfurt.'

'You look exactly like Hans.'

'Maybe I'm his double. Or maybe I'm his ghost!'

My facetious remark did not amuse the young man. He looked confused and stepped back, a look of horror spreading over his face. 'No, no,' he stammered. 'Hans is alive, you can't be his ghost!'

'I was only joking.'

But he had turned away, hurrying off through the crowd. He seemed agitated. I shrugged philosophically. So I had a double called Hans, I reflected; perhaps I too would run into him some day.

I mention this incident only to show that most of us have lookalikes, and that sometimes we see what we want to see, or are looking for, even if on looking closer, the resemblance isn't all that striking.

But there was no mistaking Kishen when he approached me. I hadn't seen him for five or six years, but he looked much the same. Bushy eyebrows, offset by gentle eyes; a determined chin, offset by a charming smile. The girls had always liked him, and he knew it; and he was content to let them do the pursuing.

We watched a film—I think it was *The Wind Cannot Read*—and then we strolled across to the old Standard Restaurant, ordered dinner and talked about old times, while the small band played sentimental tunes from the 1950s.

Yes, we talked about old times—growing up in Dehra, where we lived next door to each other, exploring our neighbours' litchi orchards, cycling about the town in the days before the scooter had been invented, kicking a football around on the maidan, or just sitting on the compound wall doing nothing. I had just finished school, and an entire year stretched before me until it was time to go abroad. Kishen's father, a civil engineer, was under transfer orders, so Kishen, too, temporarily did not have to go to school.

He was an easy-going boy, quite content to be at a loose end in my company—I was to describe a couple of our escapades in my first novel, *The Room on the Roof*. I had literary pretensions; he was apparently without ambition although, as he grew older, he was to surprise me by his wide reading and erudition.

One day, while we were cycling along the bank of the Rajpur canal, he skidded off the path and fell into the canal with his cycle. The water was only waist-deep; but it was quite swift, and I had to jump in to help him. There was no real danger, but we had some difficulty getting the cycle out of the canal.

Later, he learnt to swim.

But that was after I'd gone away . . .

Convinced that my prospects would be better in England, my mother packed me off to her relatives in Jersey, and it was to be four long years before I could return to the land I truly cared for. By that time, many of my Dehra friends had left the town; it wasn't a place where you could do much after finishing school. Kishen wrote to me from Calcutta, where he was at an engineering college. Then he was off to 'study abroad'. I heard from him from time to time. He seemed happy. He had an equable temperament and got on quite well with most people. He had a girlfriend too, he told me.

'But,' he wrote, 'you're my oldest and best friend. Wherever I go, I'll always come back to see you.'

And, of course, he did. We met several times while I was living in Delhi, and once we revisited Dehra together and walked down Rajpur Road and ate tikkis and golguppas behind the Clock Tower. But the old familiar faces were missing. The streets were overbuilt and overcrowded, and the litchi gardens were fast disappearing. After we got back to Delhi, Kishen accepted the offer of a job in Mumbai. We kept in touch in desultory fashion, but our paths and our lives had taken different directions. He was busy nurturing his career with an engineering firm; I had retreated to the hills with radically different goals—to write and be free of the burden of a ten-to-five desk job.

Time went by, and I lost track of Kishen.

About a year ago, I was standing in the lobby of the India International Centre, when an attractive young woman in her mid-thirties came up to me and said, 'Hello, Rusty, don't you remember me? I'm Manju. I lived next to you and Kishen and Ranbir when we were children.'

I recognized her then, for she had always been a pretty girl, the belle of Dehra's Astley Hall.

We sat down and talked about old times and new times, and I told her that I hadn't heard from Kishen for a few years.

'Didn't you know?' she asked. 'He died about two years ago.'

'What happened?' I was dismayed, even angry, that I hadn't heard about it. 'He couldn't have been more than thirty-eight.'

'It was an accident on a beach in Goa. A child had got into difficulties and Kishen swam out to save her. He did rescue the little girl, but when he reached the shore he had a heart attack. Kishen died right there on the beach. It seems he had always had a weak heart. The exertion must have been too much for him.'

I was silent. I knew he'd become a fairly good swimmer, but I did not know about the heart.

'Was he married?' I asked.

'No, he was always the eligible bachelor boy.'

It had been good to see Manju again, even though she had given me bad news. She told me she was happily married, with a small son. We promised to keep in touch.

And that's the end of this tale, apart from my brief visit to Delhi last November.

I had taken a taxi to Connaught Place and decided to get down at the Regal. I stood there awhile, undecided about what to do or where to go. It was almost time for a show to start, and there were a lot of people milling around.

I thought someone called my name. I looked around, and there was Kishen in the crowd.

'Kishen!' I called, and started after him.

But a stout lady climbing out of an autorickshaw got in my way, and by the time I had a clear view again, my old friend had disappeared.

Had I seen his lookalike, a double? Or had he kept his promise to come back to see me once more?

The Crooked Tree

My room in Shahganj was very small. I had paced about in it so often that I knew its exact measurements: twelve feet by ten. The string of my cot needed tightening. The dip in the middle was so pronounced that I invariably woke up in the morning with a backache; but I was hopeless at tightening charpoy strings.

Under the cot was my tin trunk. Its contents ranged from old, rejected manuscripts to clothes, letters and photographs. I had resolved that one day, when I had made some money with a book, I would throw the trunk and everything else out of the window, and leave Shahganj forever. But until then I was a prisoner. The rent was nominal, the window had a view of the bus stop and rickshaw stand, and I had nowhere else to go.

I did not live entirely alone. Sometimes a beggar spent the night on the balcony; and, during cold or wet weather, the boys from the tea shop, who normally slept on the pavement, crowded into the room.

Usually I woke early in the mornings, as sleep was fitful, uneasy, often crowded with dreams. I knew it was five o'clock when I heard the first upcountry bus leaving its shed. I would then get up and take a walk in the fields beyond the railroad tracks.

One morning, while I was walking in the fields, I noticed someone lying across the pathway, his head and shoulders hidden by the stalks of young sugar cane. When I came near, I saw he was a boy of about sixteen. His body was twitching convulsively, his face was very white, except where a little blood had trickled down his chin. His legs kept moving and his hands fluttered restlessly, helplessly.

'What's the matter with you?' I asked, kneeling down beside him.

But he was unconscious and could not answer me.

I ran down the footpath to a well and, dipping the end of my shirt in a shallow trough of water, ran back and sponged the boy's face. The twitching ceased and, though he still breathed heavily, his hands became still and his face calm. He opened his eyes and stared at me without any immediate comprehension.

'You have bitten your tongue,' I said, wiping the blood from his mouth. 'Don't worry. I'll stay with you until you feel better.'

He sat up now and spoke, 'I'm all right, thank you.'

'What happened?' I asked, sitting down beside him.

'Oh, nothing much. It often happens, I don't know why. But I cannot control it.'

'Have you seen a doctor?'

'I went to the hospital in the beginning. They gave me some pills, which I had to take every day. But the pills made me so tired and sleepy that I couldn't work properly. So I stopped taking them. Now this happens once or twice a month. But what does it matter? I'm all right when it's over, and I don't feel anything while it is happening.'

He got to his feet, dusting his clothes and smiling at me. He was slim, long-limbed and bony. There was a little fluff on his cheeks and the promise of a moustache.

'Where do you live?' I asked. 'I'll walk back with you.'

'I don't live anywhere,' he replied. 'Sometimes I sleep in the temple, sometimes in the gurdwara. In summer months I sleep in the municipal gardens.'

'Well, then let me come with you as far as the gardens.'

He told me that his name was Kamal, that he studied at the Shahganj High School, and that he hoped to pass his examinations in a few months' time. He was studying hard and, if he passed with a good division, he hoped to attend a college. If he failed, there was only the prospect of continuing to live in the municipal gardens . . .

Kamal carried with him a small tray of merchandise, supported by straps that went round his shoulders. In it were combs and buttons and cheap toys and little vials of perfume. All day he walked about Shahganj, selling odds and ends to people in the bazaar or at their houses. He made, on an average, two rupees a day, which was enough for his food and his school fees.

He told me all this while we walked back to the bus stand. I returned to my room to try and write something, while Kamal went on to the bazaar to try and sell his wares.

There was nothing very unusual about Kamal's being an orphan and a refugee. During the communal holocaust of

1947, thousands of homes had been broken up, and women and children had been killed. What was unusual in Kamal was his sensitivity, a quality I thought rare in a Punjabi youth who had grown up in the Frontier provinces during a period of hate and violence. And it was not so much his positive attitude to life that appealed to me (most people in Shahganj were completely resigned to their lot) as his gentleness, his quiet voice and the smile that flickered across his face regardless of whether he was sad or happy. In the morning, when I opened my door, I found Kamal asleep at the top of the steps. His tray lay a few feet away. I shook him gently, and he woke at once.

'Have you been sleeping here all night?' I asked. 'Why didn't you come inside?'

'It was very late,' he said. 'I didn't want to disturb you.'
'Someone could have stolen your things while you slept.'

'Oh, I sleep quite lightly. Besides, I have nothing of special value. But I came to ask you something.'

'Do you need any money?'

'No. I want you to take your meal with me tonight.'

'But where? You don't have a place of your own. It will be too expensive in a restaurant.'

'In your room,' said Kamal. 'I will bring the food and cook it here. You have a stove?'

'I think so,' I said. 'I will have to look for it.'

'I will come at seven,' said Kamal, strapping on his tray. 'Don't worry. I know how to cook!'

He ran down the steps and made for the bazaar. I began to look for the oil stove, found it at the bottom of my tin trunk,

30

and then discovered I hadn't any pots or pans or dishes. Finally, I borrowed these from Deep Chand, the barber.

Kamal brought a chicken for our dinner. This was a luxury in Shahganj, to be eaten only two or three times a year. He had bought the bird for three rupees, which was cheap, considering it was not too skinny. While Kamal set about roasting it, I went down to the bazaar and procured a bottle of beer on credit, and this served as an appetizer.

'We are having an expensive meal,' I observed. 'Three rupees for the chicken and three rupees for the beer. But I wish we could do it more often.'

'We should do it at least once a month,' said Kamal. 'It should be possible if we work hard.'

'You know how to work. You work from morning to night.'

'But you are a writer, Rusty. That is different. You have to wait for a mood.'

'Oh, I'm not a genius that I can afford the luxury of moods. No, I'm just lazy, that's all.'

'Perhaps you are writing the wrong things.'

'I know I am. But I don't know how I can write anything else.'

'Have you tried?'

'Yes, but there is no money in it. I wish I could make a living in some other way. Even if I repaired cycles, I would make more money.'

'Then why not repair cycles?'

'No, I will not repair cycles. I would rather be a bad writer than a good repairer of cycles. But let us not think of work. There is time enough for work. I want to know more about you.'

Kamal did not know if his parents were alive or dead. He had lost them, literally, when he was six. It happened at the Amritsar station, where trains coming across the border disgorged thousands of refugees, or pulled into the station half-empty, drenched with blood and littered with corpses.

Kamal and his parents were lucky to escape the massacre. Had they travelled on an earlier train (they had tried desperately to get into one), they might well have been killed; but circumstances favoured them then, only to trick them later.

Kamal was clinging to his mother's sari, while she remained close to her husband, who was elbowing his way through the frightened, bewildered throng of refugees. Glancing over his shoulder at a woman who lay on the ground, wailing and beating her breasts, Kamal collided with a burly Sikh and lost his grip on his mother's sari.

The Sikh had a long, curved sword at his waist; and Kamal stared up at him in awe and fascination—at his long hair, which had fallen loose, and his wild, black beard, and the bloodstains on his white shirt. The Sikh pushed him out of the way and when Kamal looked around for his mother, she was not to be seen. She was hidden from him by a mass of restless bodies, pushed in different directions. He could hear her calling, 'Kamal, where are you, Kamal?' He tried to force his way through the crowd, in the direction of the voice, but he was carried the other way . . .

At night, when the platform was empty, he was still searching for his mother. Eventually, some soldiers took him away. They looked for his parents, but without success, and finally, they sent Kamal to a refugee camp. From there he went to an orphanage. But when he was eight, and felt himself a man, he ran away.

He worked for some time as a helper in a tea shop; but when he started getting epileptic fits, the shopkeeper asked him to leave, and Kamal found himself on the streets, begging for a living. He begged for a year, moving from one town to another, and finally ended up at Shahganj. By then he was twelve and too old to beg; but he had saved some money, and with it he bought a small stock of combs, buttons, cheap perfumes and bangles and, converting himself into a mobile shop, went from door to door, selling his wares.

Shahganj was a small town, and there was no house which Kamal hadn't visited. Everyone recognized him, and there were some who offered him food and drink; the children knew him well, because he played on a small flute whenever he made his rounds, and they followed him to listen to the flute.

I began to look forward to Kamal's presence. He dispelled some of my own loneliness. I found I could work better, knowing that I did not have to work alone. And Kamal came to me, perhaps because I was the first person to have taken a personal interest in his life, and because I saw nothing frightening in his illness. Most people in Shahganj thought epilepsy was infectious; some considered it a form of divine punishment for sins committed in a former life. Except for children, those who knew of his condition generally gave him a wide berth.

At sixteen, a boy grows like young wheat, springing up so fast that he is unaware of what is taking place within him. His mind quickens, his gestures become more confident. Hair sprouts like young grass on his face and chest, and his muscles begin to mature. Never again will he experience so much change and growth in so short a time. He is full of currents and countercurrents.

33

Kamal combined the bloom of youth with the beauty of the short-lived. It made me sad even to look at his pale, slim body. It hurt me to look into his eyes. Life and death were always struggling in their depths.

'Should I go to Delhi and take up a job?' I asked.

'Why not? You are always talking about it.'

'Why don't you come, too? Perhaps the doctors there can stop your fits.'

'We will need money for that. When I have passed my examinations, I will come.'

'Then I will wait,' I said. I was twenty-two, and there was world enough and time for everything.

We decided to save a little money from his small earnings and my occasional payments. We would need money to go to Delhi, money to live there until we could earn a living. We put away twenty rupees one week, but lost it the next when we lent it to a friend who owned a cycle rickshaw. But this gave us the occasional use of his cycle, and early one morning, with Kamal sitting on the crossbar, I rode out of Shahganj.

After cycling for about two miles, we got down and pushed the cycle off the road, taking a path through a paddy field and then through a field of young maize, until in the distance we saw a tree, a crooked tree, growing beside an old well.

I do not know the name of that tree. I had never seen one like it before. It had a crooked trunk and crooked branches, and was clothed in thick, broad, crooked leaves, like the leaves on which food is served in the bazaar.

In the trunk of the tree there was a hole, and when we set the bicycle down with a crash, a pair of green parrots flew out, and went dipping and swerving across the fields. There was grass around the well, cropped short by grazing cattle.

We sat in the shade of the crooked tree, and Kamal untied the red cloth in which he had brought our food. When we had eaten, we stretched ourselves out on the grass. I closed my eyes and became aware of a score of different sensations. I heard a cricket singing in the tree, the cooing of pigeons from the walls of the old well, the quiet breathing of Kamal, the parrots returning to the tree, the distant hum of an airplane. I smelled the grass and the old bricks round the well and the promise of rain. I felt Kamal's fingers against my arm, and the sun creeping over my cheek. And when I opened my eyes, there were clouds on the horizon, and Kamal was asleep, his arm thrown across his face to keep out the glare.

I went to the well, and putting my shoulders to the ancient handle, turned the wheel, moving around while cool, clean water gushed out over the stones and along the channel to the fields. The discovery that I could water a field, that I had the power to make things grow, gave me a thrill of satisfaction; it was like writing a story that had a ring of truth. I drank from one of the trays; the water was sweet with age.

Kamal was sitting up, looking at the sky. 'It's going to rain,' he said.

We began cycling homeward; but we were still some way out of Shahganj when it began to rain. A lashing wind swept the rain across our faces, but we exulted in it, and sang at the top of our voices until we reached the Shahganj bus stop.

Across the railroad tracks and the dry riverbed, fields of maize stretched away, until there came a dry region of thorn bushes and lantana scrub, where the earth was cut into jagged cracks, like a jigsaw puzzle. Dotting the landscape were old, abandoned brick kilns. When it rained heavily, the hollows filled up with water.

Kamal and I came to one of these hollows to bathe and swim. There was an island in the middle of it, and on this small mound lay the ruins of a hut where a nightwatchman, who looked after the brick kilns, had once lived. We would swim out to the island, which was only a few yards from the banks of the hollow. There was a grassy patch in front of the hut, and early in the mornings, before it got too hot, we would wrestle on the grass.

Though I was heavier than Kamal, my chest as sound as a new drum, he had strong, wiry arms and legs, and would often pinion me around the waist with his bony knees. Now, while we wrestled on the new monsoon grass, I felt his body go tense. He stiffened, his legs jerked against my body, and a shudder passed through him. I knew that he had a fit coming on, but I was unable to extricate myself from his arms.

He gripped me more tightly as the fit took possession of him. Instead of struggling, I lay still, tried to absorb some of his anguish, tried to draw some of his agitation to myself. I had a strange fancy that by identifying myself with his convulsions, I might alleviate them.

I pressed against Kamal, and whispered soothingly into his ear, and then, when I noticed his mouth working, I thrust my fingers between his teeth to prevent him from biting his tongue. But so violent was the convulsion that his teeth bit into the flesh of my palm and ground against my knuckles. I shouted with the pain and tried to jerk my hand away, but it was impossible to loosen the grip of his jaws. So I closed my eyes and counted— counted till seven—until consciousness returned to him and his muscles relaxed. My hand was shaking and covered with blood. I bound it in my handkerchief and kept it hidden from Kamal.

We walked back to the room without talking much. Kamal looked depressed and weak. I kept my hand beneath my shirt, and Kamal was too dejected to notice anything. It was only at night, when he returned from his classes, that he noticed the cuts, and I told him I had slipped on the road, cutting my hand on some broken glass.

The rains came upon Shahganj. And, until the rain stops, Shahganj is fresh and clean and alive. The children run out of their houses, glorying in their nakedness. The gutters choke, and the narrow street becomes a torrent of water, coursing merrily down to the bus stop. It swirls over the trees and the roofs of the town, and the parched earth soaks it up, exuding a fragrance that comes only once in a year, the fragrance of quenched earth, that most exhilarating of smells.

The rain swept in through the door and soaked the cot. When I had succeeded in closing the door, I found the roof leaking, the water trickling down the walls and forming new pictures on the cracking plaster. The door flew open again, and there was Kamal standing on the threshold, shaking himself like a wet dog. Coming in, he stripped and dried himself, and then sat shivering on the bed while I made frantic efforts to close the door again.

'You need some tea,' I said.

He nodded, forgetting to smile for once, and I knew his mind was elsewhere, in one of a hundred possible places from his dreams.

'One day I will write a book,' I said, as we drank strong tea in the fast-fading twilight. 'A real book, about real people.

37

Perhaps it will be about you and me and Shahganj. And then we will run away from Shahganj, fly on the wings of Garuda, and all our troubles will be over and fresh troubles will begin. Why should we mind difficulties, as long as they are new difficulties?'

'First I must pass my exams,' said Kamal. 'Otherwise, I can do nothing, go nowhere.'

'Don't take exams too seriously. I know that in India they are the passport to any kind of job, and that you cannot become a clerk unless you have a degree. But do not forget that you are studying for the sake of acquiring knowledge, and not for the sake of becoming a clerk. You don't want to become a clerk or a bus conductor, do you? You must pass your exams and go to college, but do not feel that if you fail, you will be able to do nothing. Why, you can start making your own buttons instead of selling other people's!'

'You are right,' said Kamal. 'But why not be an educated button manufacturer?'

'Why not, indeed? That's just what I mean. And, while you are studying for your exams, I will be writing my book. I will start tonight!

It is an auspicious night, the beginning of the monsoon. The light did not come on. A tree must have fallen across the wires. I lit a candle and placed it on the windowsill and, while the candle spluttered in the steamy air, Kamal opened his books and, with one hand on a book and the other hand playing with his toes—this attitude helped him to concentrate—he devoted his attention to algebra.

I took an ink bottle down from a shelf and, finding it empty, added a little rainwater to the crusted contents. Then

I sat down beside Kamal and began to write; but the pen was useless and made blotches all over the paper, and I had no idea what I should write about, though I was full of writing just then. So I began to look at Kamal instead, at his eyes, hidden in shadow, and his hands, quiet in the candlelight; and I followed his breathing and the slight movement of his lips as he read softly to himself.

And, instead of starting my book, I sat and watched Kamal.

Sometimes Kamal played the flute at night, while I was lying awake; and, even when I was asleep, the flute would play in my dreams. Sometimes he brought it to the crooked tree, and played it for the benefit of the birds; but the parrots only made harsh noises and flew away.

Once, when Kamal was playing his flute to a group of children, he had a fit. The flute fell from his hands, and he began to roll about in the dust on the roadside. The children were frightened and ran away. But the next time they heard Kamal play his flute, they came to listen as usual.

That Kamal was gaining in strength I knew from the way he was able to pin me down whenever we wrestled on the grass near the old brick kilns. It was no longer necessary for me to yield deliberately to him. And, though his fits still recurred from time to time—as we knew they would continue to do—he was not so depressed afterwards. The anxiety and the death had gone from his eyes.

His examinations were nearing, and he was working hard. (I had yet to begin the first chapter of my book.) Because of the necessity of selling two or three rupees' worth of articles every day, he did not get much time for studying; but he stuck to his books until past midnight, and it was seldom that I heard his flute.

He put aside his tray of odds and ends during the examinations, and walked to the examination centre instead. And after two weeks, when it was all over, he took up his tray and began his rounds again. In a burst of creativity, I wrote three pages of my novel.

On the morning the results of the examination were due, I rose early, before Kamal, and went down to the news agency. It was five o'clock and the newspapers had just arrived. I went through the columns relating to Shahganj, but I couldn't find Kamal's roll number on the list of successful candidates. I had the number written down on a slip of paper, and I looked at it again to make sure that I had compared it correctly with the others; then I went through the newspaper once more.

When I returned to the room, Kamal was sitting on the doorstep. I didn't have to tell him he had failed. He knew by the look on my face. I sat down beside him, and we said nothing for some time.

'Never mind,' said Kamal, eventually. 'I will pass next year.' I realized that I was more depressed than he was, and that he was trying to console me.

'If only you'd had more time,' I said.

'I have plenty of time now. Another year. And you will have time in which to finish your book; then we can both go away. Another year of Shahganj won't be so bad. As long as I have your friendship, almost everything else can be tolerated, even my sickness.'

And then, turning to me with an expression of intense happiness, he said, 'Yesterday I was sad, and tomorrow I may be sad again, but today I know that I am happy. I want to live on and on. I feel that life isn't long enough to satisfy me.'

He stood up, the tray hanging from his shoulders.

'What would you like to buy?' he said. 'I have everything you need.'

At the bottom of the steps he turned and smiled at me, and I knew then that I had written my story.

My Best Friend

My best friend
Is the baker's son,
I gave him a book
And he gave me a bun!

I told him a tale
Of a magical lake,
And he liked it so much
That he baked me a cake.

Yes, he's my best friend—
We go cycling together,
On bright sunny days,
And in rain and bad weather.

And if we feel hungry
There's always a pie
Or a pastry to feast on,
As we go riding by!

A Little Friend

When I first arrived in London I knew no one. I was eighteen and on my own; looking for a room, looking for a job. I spent a week in a students' hostel, a noisy place full of foreign students talking in every tongue except English. Then I saw an ad for a room to let, for just a pound a week. I was on the dole, getting just three pounds a week, so I took the room without even looking at it.

It turned out to be a tiny attic at the top of the building. Nothing above me but a low ceiling and a slanting tiled roof. There was a bed, a small dressing table, and a gas fire in the corner of the room. You had to shove several pennies into a slot before you could light the fire. It was November, very cold, and I kept running out of pennies. The toilet was about two floors below me. Above the potty was a notice which said 'Do not throw your tea leaves in here.' As I did not have anything to cook on, I had no tea leaves to deposit in the loo. I supposed that the other tenants (whom I seldom saw) were given to flushing away their tea leaves.

My landlady was Jewish, and I did not see much of her either, except when the rent was due. She was a Polish refugee, and I think she'd had a hard time in Europe during the War. It was seldom that she emerged from her room.

There was no bath in the building, I had to use the public baths some way down Belsize Road. I took my meals, the cheapest I could get, at a snack bar near the underground station. Some evenings I would bring home a loaf of bread and a tin of sardines; *this* was luxury.

Was I lonely? You can bet I was . . . terribly lonely. I had no friends in that great city. Even the city looked lonely, all grey and fogbound. Every day I visited the employment exchange, and after two weeks I landed a job as a ledger clerk in a large grocery store. The pay was five pounds a week.

I was rich! For once I could have a proper lunch instead of the usual beans on toast. I bought ham and cheese and celebrated with sandwiches and a bottle of cheap sherry. Soon there were crumbs all over the floor of my room. My landlady wouldn't like that. I was about to get up to sweep them away when there was a squeak and a little mouse ran across the floor with a bit of cheese that it had found. He darted across the room and disappeared behind the dressing table.

I decided not to clear away the crumbs; let the mouse have them. 'Waste not, want not,' as my grandmother used to say.

I did not see the mouse again, but after I'd put the light out and gone to bed, I could hear him scurrying about the room, collecting titbits. Now and then he emitted a little squeak, possibly of satisfaction.

'Well, at least I did not have to celebrate alone,' I said to myself, 'a mouse for company is better than no company at all.'

I was off to work early next morning, and in my absence my landlady had my room cleaned. I came back to find a note on the dressing table which said: 'Please do not scatter food on the floor.'

She was right, of course. My room-mate deserved better than a scattering of crumbs. So I provided him with an empty soap dish, which I placed near the dressing table, and I filled it with an assortment of biscuit crumbs. But for some reason he wouldn't go near the soap dish. I stayed up quite late, waiting for him to appear, and when he did, he explored all corners of the room and even approached my bed, but stayed well away from the soap dish. Perhaps he didn't like the colour, a bright pink. I've been told by a scientist that mice are colour-blind and wouldn't be able to distinguish a pink soap dish from a blue one. But I think the scientist got it wrong. Quite often, they do.

I couldn't tell if my mouse was a male or a female, but for some indefinable reason I felt that he was a bachelor, like me. Surely a female mouse would be living with her family. This one was very much a loner.

I threw the soap dish away, and the following evening, on my way home from work, I bought a pretty little saucer, and this I placed near his residence, with a piece of cheese in the middle. He came to it almost instantly, nibbled at the cheese, approved of it, and carried the rest of it back to his hole behind the dressing table.

A fussy mouse! No soap dish for him. He had to have a saucer with a Chinese willow-pattern design.

After some time we become protective of our own. Summer came to London early in May, and finding the room stuffier than usual, I opened the small window that looked out upon a sea of rooftops, all similar to ours and to each other. But I could not leave it open for long. Suddenly I heard an agitated squeak from below my bed, and the mouse scurried across the room to the safety of the dressing table. Looking up, I saw a large tabby cat framed in the open window, looking in with a speculative air. I think he had seen, or sensed, that there was a free lunch in the offing if he was patient enough.

'No free lunches for cats,' I said, and closed the window and kept it shut.

On weekends I roamed the city, occasionally visiting suburban cinemas where the seats were cheap; but on weekdays I'd stay at home in the evenings, working on my novel, my romance of India, and occasionally reading aloud from my manuscript.

The mouse wasn't a very good listener, he was never long in one place, but he was now trusting enough to take a piece of cheese or bread from my fingers, and if I spent too much time on my book, he would remind me of his presence by giving several little squeaks—scolding me for not paying attention to his needs.

Alas, the time came when I had to consider parting from the 'Lone Ranger', as I had come to call my fellow lodger. A slight increase in salary, and a cheque from BBC radio for a couple of stories, meant I could move to bigger and better lodgings in a more congenial area of London. My landlady was sorry to see me go, for, in spite of my untidy ways, I had been regular with the rent. And the little mouse—would he too be sorry to see me go? He would have to forage further afield for his meals. And the next tenant might prefer cats to mice!

This was my worry, not his. Unlike humans, mice don't worry about the future—their own or the world's.

The problem was partly resolved by the arrival of another tenant—not a human tenant, but another mouse, presumably a female, because she was a little smaller and a little prettier than my room-mate. Two or three days before I was to leave, I came home to find them chasing each other about the room with a great deal of squeaking and acrobatic play. Was this romance?

I felt a twinge of envy. My little friend had found a companion, and I was still without one. But when the time came for me to leave, I made sure they were well supplied with an assortment of crackers and rusks—enough to last well over a month, provided our landlady did not find them first.

I packed my battered old suitcase and left that small attic behind. As we journey through life, old friends and new friends, are often left behind, never to be met with again. There are times when we are on our own, lonely, in need of a friendly presence. Just someone to be there when we return to that empty, joyless room. And at such times, even a little mouse, can make a big difference.

The Thief

I was still a thief when I met Arun, and though I was only fifteen I was an experienced and fairly successful hand.

Arun was watching the wrestlers when I approached him. He was about twenty, a tall, lean fellow, and he looked kind and simple enough for my purpose. I hadn't had much luck of late and thought I might be able to get into this young person's confidence. He seemed quite fascinated by the wrestling. Two well-oiled men slid about in the soft mud, grunting and slapping their thighs. When I drew Arun into conversation, he didn't seem to realize I was a stranger.

'You look like a wrestler yourself,' I said.

'So do you,' he replied, which put me out of my stride for a moment, because at the time I was rather thin and bony and not very impressive physically.

'Yes,' I admitted. 'I wrestle sometimes.'

'What's your name?'

'Deepak,' I lied.

Deepak was about my fifth name. I had earlier called myself Ranbir, Sudhir, Trilok and Surinder.

After this preliminary exchange Arun confined himself to comments on the match, and I didn't have much to say. After a while he walked away from the crowd of spectators. I followed him.

'Hello,' he said. 'Enjoying yourself?'

I gave him my most appealing smile. 'I want to work for you,' I said.

He didn't stop walking. 'And what makes you think I want someone to work for me?'

'Well,' I continued, 'I've been wandering about all day looking for the best person to work for. When I saw you I knew that no one else had a chance.'

'You flatter me,' he said.

'That's all right.'

'But you can't work for me.'

'Why not?'

'Because I can't pay you.'

I thought that over for a minute. Perhaps I had misjudged my man.

'Can you feed me?' I asked.

'Can you cook?' he countered.

'I can cook,' I lied.

'If you can cook,' he said, 'I'll feed you.'

He took me to his room and told me I could sleep on the veranda. But I was nearly back on the street that same night. The meal I cooked must have been pretty awful, because Arun gave it to the neighbour's cat and told me to be off. But I just hung around smiling in my most appealing way, and then he couldn't help laughing. He sat down on the bed and laughed for a full five minutes and later patted me on the head and said, never mind, he'd teach me to cook in the morning.

Not only did he teach me to cook but he taught me to write my name and his, and said he would soon teach me to write whole sentences and add money on paper when you didn't have any in your pocket!

It was quite pleasant working for Arun. I made the tea in the morning and later went out shopping. I would take my time buying the day's supplies and make a profit of about twenty-five paise a day. I would tell Arun that rice was fifty-six paise a pound (it generally was), but I would get it at fifty paise a pound. I think he knew that I made a little this way but he didn't mind. He wasn't giving me a regular wage.

I was really grateful to Arun for teaching me to write. I knew that once I could write like an educated man, there would be no limit to what I could achieve. It might even be an incentive to be honest.

Arun made money by fits and starts. He would be borrowing one week, lending the next. He would keep worrying about his next cheque, but as soon as it arrived he would go out and celebrate lavishly.

One evening he came home with a wad of notes, and at night I saw him tuck the bundles under his mattress at the head of the bed.

I had been working for Arun for nearly a fortnight and, apart from the shopping, hadn't done much to exploit him. I had every opportunity for doing so. I had a key to the front door which meant I had access to the room whenever Arun was out. He was the most trusting person I had ever met. And that was why I couldn't make up my mind to rob him.

It's easy to rob a greedy man because he deserves to be robbed. It's easy to rob a rich man because he can afford to be robbed. But it's difficult to rob a poor man, even one who really doesn't care if he's robbed. A rich man or a greedy man or a careful man wouldn't keep his money under a pillow or mattress. He'd lock it up in a safe place. Arun had put his money where it would be child's play for me to remove it without his knowledge.

It's time I did some real work, I told myself. I'm getting out of practice . . . If I don't take the money, he'll only waste it on his friends . . . He doesn't even pay me . . .

Arun was asleep. Moonlight came in from the veranda and fell across the bed. I sat up on the floor, my blanket wrapped round me, considering the situation. There was quite a lot of money in that wad and if I took it I would have to leave town—I might make the ten-thirty express to Amritsar . . .

Slipping out of the blanket, I crept on all fours through the door up to the bed and peeped at Arun. He was sleeping peacefully with a soft and easy breathing. His face was clear and unlined. Even I had more markings on my face, though mine were mostly scars.

My hand took on an identity of its own as it slid around under the mattress, the fingers searching for the bundle. They found the notes and I drew them out without a crackle.

Arun sighed in his sleep and turned on his side, towards me. My free hand was resting on the bed and his hair touched my fingers.

I was frightened when his hair touched my fingers. Quickly and quietly, I crawled out of the room.

When I was in the street I began to run. I ran down the bazaar road to the station. The shops were all closed but a few lights were on in the upper windows. I had the notes at my waist, held there by the string of my pyjamas. I felt I had to stop and count the notes, though I knew it might make me late for the train. It was already ten-twenty by the Clock Tower. I slowed down to a walk and my fingers flicked through the notes. There were about a hundred rupees in fives. A good haul. I could live like a prince for a month or two.

When I reached the station, I did not stop at the ticket office (I had never bought a ticket in my life) but dashed straight on to the platform. The Amritsar Express was just pulling out. It was moving slowly enough for me to be able to jump on the footboard of one of the carriages, but I hesitated for some urgent, unexplainable reason.

I hesitated long enough for the train to leave without me.

When it had gone and the noise and busy confusion of the platform had subsided, I found myself standing alone on the deserted platform. The knowledge that I had a hundred stolen rupees in my pyjamas only increased my feeling of isolation and loneliness. I had no idea where to spend the night. I had never kept any friends because sometimes friends can be one's undoing. I didn't want to make myself conspicuous by staying at a hotel. And the only person I knew really well in town was the person I had robbed!

Leaving the station, I walked slowly through the bazaar keeping to dark, deserted alleys. I kept thinking of Arun. He would still be asleep, blissfully unaware of his loss.

I have made a study of men's faces when they have lost something of material value. The greedy man shows panic, the rich man shows anger, the poor man shows fear. But I knew that neither panic nor anger nor fear would show on Arun's face when he discovered the theft, only a terrible sadness, not for the loss of the money but for me having betrayed his trust.

I found myself on the maidan and sat down on a bench with my feet tucked up under my haunches. The night was a little cold and I regretted not having brought Arun's blanket along. A light drizzle added to my discomfort. Soon it was raining heavily. My shirt and pyjamas stuck to my skin, and a cold wind brought the rain whipping across my face. I told myself that sleeping on a bench was something I should have been used to by now, but the veranda had softened me.

I walked back to the bazaar and sat down on the steps of a closed shop. A few vagrants lay beside me, rolled up tight in thin blankets. The clock showed midnight. I felt for the notes. They were still with me but had lost their crispness and were damp with rainwater.

Arun's money. In the morning he would probably have given me a rupee to go to the pictures, but now I had it all. No more cooking his meals, running to the bazaar, or learning to write whole sentences. Whole sentences . . .

They were something I had forgotten in the excitement of a hundred rupees. Whole sentences, I knew, could one day bring me more than a hundred rupees. It was a simple matter to steal (and sometimes just as simple to be caught) but to be a really big man, a wise and successful man, that was something. I should go back to Arun, I told myself, if only to learn how to write.

Perhaps it was also concern for Arun that drew me back. A sense of sympathy is one of my weaknesses, and through hesitation over a theft I had often been caught. A successful thief must be pitiless. I was fond of Arun. My affection for him, my sense of sympathy, but most of all my desire to write whole sentences, drew me back to the room.

I hurried back extremely nervous, for it is easier to steal something than to return it undetected. If I was caught beside the bed now, with the money in my hand, or with my hand under the mattress, there could be only one explanation: that I was actually stealing. If Arun woke up I would be lost.

I opened the door clumsily and stood in the doorway in clouded moonlight. Gradually my eyes became accustomed to the darkness of the room. Arun was still asleep. I went on all fours again and crept noiselessly to the head of the bed. My hand came up with the notes. I felt his breath on my fingers. I was fascinated by his tranquil features and easy breathing, and remained motionless for a minute. Then my hand explored the mattress, found the edge, slipped under it with the notes.

I awoke late next morning to find that Arun had already made the tea. I found it difficult to face him in the harsh light of day. His hand was stretched out towards me. There was a five-rupee note between his fingers. My heart sank.

'I made some money yesterday,' he said. 'Now you'll get paid regularly.' My spirit rose as rapidly as it had fallen. I congratulated myself on having returned the money.

But when I took the note, I realized that he knew everything.

The note was still wet from last night's rain.

The Thief

'Today I'll teach you to write a little more than your name,' he said.

Arun knew but neither his lips nor his eyes said anything about their knowing.

I smiled at Arun in my most appealing way. And the smile came by itself, without my knowing it.

Most Beautiful

I don't quite know why I found that particular town so heartless. Perhaps because of its crowded, claustrophobic atmosphere, its congested and insanitary lanes, its weary people . . . One day I found the children of the bazaar tormenting a deformed, retarded boy.

About a dozen boys, between the ages of eight and fourteen, were jeering at the retard, who was making things worse for himself by confronting the gang and shouting abuses at them. The boy was twelve or thirteen, judging by his face, but had the height of an eight or nine-year-old. His legs were thick, short and bowed. He had a small chest but his arms were long, making him rather apelike in his attitude. His forehead and cheeks were pitted with the scars of smallpox. He was ugly by normal standards, and the gibberish he spoke did nothing to discourage his tormentors. They threw mud and stones at him, while keeping well out of his reach. Few can be more cruel than a gang of schoolboys in high spirits.

I was an uneasy observer of the scene. I felt that I ought to do something to put a stop to it, but lacked the courage to interfere. It was only when a stone struck the boy on the face, cutting open his cheek, that I lost my normal discretion and ran in amongst the gang, shouting at them and clouting those I could reach.

They scattered like defeated soldiery.

I was surprised at my own daring, and rather relieved when the boys did not return. I took the frightened, angry boy by the hand, and asked him where he lived. He drew away from me, but I held on to his fat, little fingers and told him I would take him home. He mumbled something incoherent and pointed down a narrow lane.

I led him away from the bazaar.

I said very little to the boy because it was obvious that he had some defect of speech. When he stopped outside a door set in a high wall, I presumed that we had come to his house.

The door was opened by a young woman. The boy immediately threw his arms around her and burst into tears. I had not been prepared for the boy's mother. Not only did she look perfectly normal physically, but she was also strikingly handsome. She must have been about thirty-five.

She thanked me for bringing her son home, and asked me into the house. The boy withdrew into a corner of the sitting room, and sat on his haunches in gloomy silence, his bow legs looking even more grotesque in this posture. His mother offered me tea, but I asked instead for a glass of water. She told the boy to fetch it, and he did so, thrusting the glass into my hands without looking me in the face.

'Suresh is my only child,' she said. 'My husband is disappointed in him, but I love my son. Do you think he is very ugly?'

'Ugly is just a word,' I answered. 'Like beauty. They mean different things to different people. What did the poet say?—

57

"Beauty is truth, truth is beauty." But if beauty and truth are the same thing, why have different words? There are no absolutes except birth and death.'

The boy squatted down at her feet, cradling his head in her lap. With the end of her sari, she began wiping his face.

'Have you tried teaching him to talk properly?' I asked.

'He has been like this since childhood. The doctors can do nothing.'

While we were talking the father came in, and the boy slunk away to the kitchen. The man thanked me curtly for bringing the boy home, and seemed at once to dismiss the whole matter from his mind. He appeared to be preoccupied with business matters. I got the impression that he had long since resigned himself to having a deformed child, and his early disappointment had changed to indifference. When I got up to leave, his wife accompanied me to the front door.

'Please do not mind if my husband is a little rude,' she said. 'His business is not going too well. If you would like to come again, please do. Suresh does not meet many people who treat him like a normal person.'

I knew that I wanted to visit them again—more out of sympathy for the mother than out of pity for the boy. But I realized that she was not interested in me personally, except as a possible mentor for her son.

After about a week I went to the house again.

Suresh's father was away on a business trip, and I stayed for lunch. The boy's mother made some delicious parathas stuffed with ground radish, and served them with pickle and curd. If Suresh ate like an animal, gobbling his food, I was not far behind him. His mother encouraged him to overeat. Suresh was morose and uncommunicative when he ate, but when I suggested that he come with me for a walk, he glanced up eagerly. At the same time a look of fear passed across his mother's face.

'Will it be all right?' she asked. 'You have seen how other children treat him. That day he slipped out of the house without telling anyone.'

'We won't go towards the bazaar,' I said. 'I was thinking of a walk in the fields.'

Suresh made encouraging noises and thumped the table with his fists to show that he wanted to go. Finally his mother consented, and the boy and I set off down the road.

He could not walk very fast because of his awkward legs, but this gave me a chance to point out to him anything that I thought might arouse his interest—parrots squabbling in a banyan tree, buffaloes wallowing in a muddy pond, a group of hermaphrodite musicians strolling down the road. Suresh took a keen interest in the hermaphrodites, perhaps because they were grotesque in their own way: tall, masculine-looking people dressed in women's garments, ankle bells jingling on their heavy feet, and their long, gaunt faces made up with rouge and mascara. For the first time, I heard Suresh laugh. Apparently he had discovered that there were human beings even odder than he. And like any human being, he lost no time in deriding them.

'Don't laugh,' I said. 'They were born that way, just as you were born the way you are.'

But he did not take me seriously and grinned, his wide mouth revealing surprisingly strong teeth.

We reached the dry riverbed on the outskirts of the town and crossing it entered a field of yellow mustard flowers. The mustard stretched away towards the edge of a subtropical forest. Seeing trees in the distance, Suresh began to run towards them, shouting and clapping his hands. He had never been out of town before. The courtyard of his house and, occasionally, the road to the bazaar, were all that he had seen of the world. Now the trees beckoned him.

We found a small stream running through the forest and I took off my clothes and leapt into the cool water, inviting Suresh to join me. He hesitated about taking off his clothes, but after watching me for a while, his eagerness to join me overcame his self-consciousness, and he exposed his misshapen little body to the soft, spring sunshine.

He waded clumsily towards me. The water which came only to my knees reached up to his chest.

'Come, I'll teach you to swim,' I called. And lifting him up from the waist, I held him afloat. He spluttered and thrashed around, but stopped struggling when he found that he could stay afloat.

Later, sitting on the banks of the stream, he discovered a small turtle sitting over a hole in the ground in which it had laid its eggs. He had never seen a turtle before, and watched it in fascination, while it drew its head into its shell and then thrust it out again with extreme circumspection. He must have felt that the turtle resembled him in some respects, with its squat legs, rounded back, and tendency to hide its head from the world.

After that I went to Suresh's house about twice a week, and we nearly always visited the stream. Before long he was able to swim a short distance. Knowing how to swim—this was something the bazaar boys never learnt—gave him a certain confidence, made his life something more than a one-dimensional existence.

The more I saw Suresh, the less conscious was I of his deformities. For me, he was fast becoming the norm, while the children of the bazaar seemed abnormal in their very similarity to each other. That he was still conscious of his ugliness—and how could he ever cease to be—was made clear to me about two months after our first meeting.

We were coming home through the mustard fields, which had turned from yellow to green, when I noticed that we were being followed by a small goat. It appeared to have been separated from its mother, and now attached itself to us. Though I tried driving the kid away, it continued tripping along at our heels, and when Suresh found that it persisted in accompanying us, he picked it up and took it home.

The kid became his main obsession during the next few days. He fed it with his own hands and allowed it to sleep at the foot of his bed. It was a pretty little kid, with fairy horns and an engaging habit of doing a hop, skip and jump when moving about the house. Everyone admired the pet, and the boy's mother and I both remarked on how pretty it was.

Suresh's resentment against the animal began to show when others started admiring it. He suspected that they found it better looking than its owner. I remember finding him squatting in front of a low mirror, holding the kid in his arms, and studying their reflections in the glass. After a few minutes of this, Suresh thrust the goat away. When he noticed that I was watching him, he got up and left the room without looking at me.

Two days later, when I called at the house, I found his mother looking very upset. I could see that she had been crying. But she seemed relieved to see me, and took me into the sitting room.

When Suresh saw me, he got up from the floor and ran to the veranda.

'What's wrong?' I asked.

'It was the little goat,' she said. 'Suresh killed it.'

She told me how the boy, in a sudden and uncontrollable rage, had thrown a brick at the kid, breaking its skull. What had upset her more than the animal's death was the fact that Suresh had shown no regret for what he had done.

'I'll talk to him,' I offered, and went out to the veranda, but the boy had disappeared.

'He must have gone to the bazaar,' said his mother anxiously. 'He does that when he's upset. Sometimes I think he likes to be teased and beaten.'

He was not in the bazaar. I found him near the stream, lying flat on his belly in the soft mud, chasing tadpoles with a stick.

'Why did you kill the goat?' I asked.

He shrugged his shoulders.

'Did you enjoy killing it?'

He looked at me and smiled and nodded his head vigorously.

'How very cruel,' I said. But I did not mean it. I knew that his cruelty was no different from mine or anyone else's; only his was an untrammelled cruelty, primitive, as yet undisguised by civilizing restraints.

He took a penknife from his shirt pocket, opened it, and held it out to me by the blade. He pointed to his bare stomach and motioned me to thrust the blade into his belly. He had such a mournful look on his face (the result of having offended me and not in remorse for the goat sacrifice) that I had to burst out laughing.

'You are a funny fellow,' I said, taking the knife from him and throwing it into the stream. 'Come, let's have a swim.'

We swam all afternoon, and Suresh went home smiling. His mother and I conspired to keep the whole affair a secret from his father—who had not in any case been aware of the goat's presence.

Suresh seemed quite contented during the following weeks. And then I received a letter offering me a job in Delhi and I knew that I would have to take it, as I was earning very little by my writing at the time.

The boy's mother was disappointed, even depressed, when I told her I would be going away. I think she had grown quite fond of me. But the boy, always unpredictable, displayed no feeling at all. I felt a little hurt by his apparent indifference. Did our weeks of companionship mean nothing to him? I told myself that he probably did not realize that he might never see me again.

On the evening my train was to leave, I went to the house to say goodbye. The boy's mother made me promise to write to them, but Suresh seemed cold and distant, and refused to sit near me or take my hand. He made me feel that I was an outsider again—one of the mob throwing stones at odd and frightening people.

At eight o'clock that evening I entered a third-class compartment and, after a brief scuffle with several other travellers, succeeded in securing a seat near a window. It enabled me to look down the length of the platform.

The guard had blown his whistle and the train was about to leave when I saw Suresh standing near the station turnstile, looking up and down the platform.

'Suresh!' I shouted and he heard me and came hobbling along the platform. He had run through the bazaar during the busiest hour of the evening.

'I'll be back next year,' I called.

The train had begun moving out of the station, and as I waved to Suresh, he broke into a stumbling run, waving his arms in frantic, restraining gestures.

I saw him stumble against someone's bedding roll and fall sprawling on the ground. The engine picked up speed and the platform receded.

And that was the last I saw of Suresh, lying alone on the crowded platform, alone in the great, grey darkness of the world, crooked and bent and twisted—the most beautiful boy in the world.

The Flute Player

Down the main road passed big yellow buses, cars, pony-drawn tongas, motorcycles and bullock carts. This steady flow of traffic seemed, somehow, to form a barrier between the city on one side of the Trunk Road, and the distant sleepy villages on the other. It seemed to cut India in half—the India Kamla knew slightly, and the India she had never seen.

Kamla's grandmother lived on the outskirts of the city of Jaipur, and just across the road from the house there were fields and villages stretching away for hundreds of miles. But Kamla had never been across the main road. It separated the busy city from the flat, green plains stretching endlessly towards the horizon.

Kamla was used to city life. In England, it was London and Manchester. In India, it was Delhi and Jaipur. Rainy Manchester was, of course, different in many ways from sun-drenched Jaipur, and Indian cities had stronger smells and more vibrant colours than their English counterparts. Nevertheless, they had much in common—busy people always on the move, money constantly changing hands, buses to catch, schools to attend, parties to go to, TV to watch. Kamla had seen very little of the English countryside, even less of India outside the cities.

Kamla's parents lived in Manchester where her father was a doctor in a large hospital. She went to school in England. But this year, during the summer holidays, she had come to India to stay with her grandmother. Apart from a maidservant and a grizzled old nightwatchman, Grandmother lived quite alone in a small house on the outskirts of Jaipur. During the winter months, Jaipur's climate was cool and bracing but in the summer, a fierce sun poured down upon the city from a cloudless sky.

None of the other city children ventured across the main road into the fields of millet, wheat and cotton, but Kamla was determined to visit the fields before she returned to England. From the flat roof of the house she could see them stretching away for miles, the ripening wheat swaying in the hot wind. Finally, when there were only two days left before she went to Delhi to board a plane for London, she made up her mind and crossed the main road.

She did this in the afternoon, when Grandmother was asleep and the servants were at the bazaar. She slipped out of the back door and her slippers kicked up dust as she ran down the path to the main road. A bus roared past and more dust rose from the road and swirled about her. Kamla ran through the dust, past the jacaranda trees that lined the road, and into the fields.

Suddenly, the world became an enormous place, bigger and more varied than it had seemed from the air, also mysterious and exciting—and just a little frightening.

The sea of wheat stretched away till it merged with the hot blinding blue of the sky. Far to her left were a few trees and the low, white huts of a village. To her right lay hollow pits of red dust and a blackened chimney where bricks used to be made. In front, some distance away, Kamla could see a camel moving round a well, drawing up water for the fields. She set out in the direction of the camel.

Her grandmother had told her not to wander off on her own in the city; but this wasn't the city, and as far as she knew, camels did not attack people.

It took her a long time to get to the camel. It was about half a mile away, though it seemed much nearer. And when Kamla reached it, she was surprised to find that there was no one else in sight. The camel was turning the wheel by itself, moving round and round the well, while the water kept gushing up in little trays to run down the channels into the fields. The camel took no notice of Kamla, did not look at her even once, just carried on about its business.

There must be someone here, thought Kamla, walking towards a mango tree that grew a few yards away. Ripe mangoes dangled like globules of gold from its branches. Under the tree, fast asleep, was a boy.

All he wore was a pair of dirty, white shorts. His body had been burnt dark by the sun; his hair was tousled, his feet chalky with dust. In the palm of his outstretched hand was a flute. He was a thin boy, with long, bony legs, but Kamla felt that he was strong too, for his body was hard and wiry.

Kamla came nearer to the sleeping boy, peering at him with some curiosity, for she had not seen a village boy before. Her shadow fell across his face. The boy woke up. He opened his eyes and stared at Kamla. When she did not say anything, he sat up, his head a little to one side, his hands clasping his knees, and stared at her.

'Who are you?' he asked a little gruffly. He was not used to waking up and finding strange girls staring at him.

'I'm Kamla. I've come from England, but I'm really from India. I mean I've come home to India, but I'm really from England.'

This was getting to be rather confusing, so she countered with an abrupt 'Who are you?'

'I'm the strongest boy in the village,' answered the boy, deciding to assert himself without any more ado. 'My name is Romi. I can wrestle and swim and climb any tree.'

'And do you sleep a lot?' asked Kamla innocently.

Romi scratched his head and grinned.

'I look after the camel,' he said. 'It is no use staying awake for the camel. It keeps going round the well until it is tired, and then it stops. When it has rested, it starts going round again. It can carry on like that all day. But it eats a lot.'

Mention of the camel's food reminded Romi that he was hungry. He was growing fast these days and was nearly always hungry. There were some mangoes lying beside him, and he offered one to Kamla. They were silent for a few minutes. You cannot suck mangoes and talk at the same time. After they had finished, they washed their hands in the water from one of the trays.

'There are parrots in the tree,' said Kamla, noticing three or four green parrots conducting a noisy meeting in the topmost branches. They reminded her a bit of a pop group she had seen and heard at home.

'They spoil most of the mangoes,' said Romi.

He flung a stone at them and missed, but they took off with

squawks of protest, flashes of green and gold wheeling in the sunshine.

'Where do you swim?' asked Kamla. 'Down in the well?'

'Of course not. I'm not a frog. There is a canal not far from here. Come, I will show you!'

As they crossed the fields, a pair of blue jays flew out of a bush, rockets of bright blue that dipped and swerved, rising and falling as they chased each other.

Remembering a story that Grandmother had told her, Kamla said, 'They are sacred birds, aren't they? Because of their blue throats.' She told him the story of the God Shiva having a blue throat because he had swallowed a poison that would have destroyed the world; he had kept the poison in his throat and would not let it go further. 'And so his throat is blue, like the blue jay's.'

Romi liked this story. His respect for Kamla greatly increased. But he was not to be outdone, and when a small grey squirrel dashed across the path he told her that squirrels, too, were sacred. Krishna, the god who had been born into a farmer's family like Romi's, had been fond of squirrels and would take them in his arms and stroke them. 'That is why squirrels have four dark lines down their backs,' concluded Romi. 'Krishna was very dark, as dark as I am, and the stripes are the marks of his fingers.'

'Can you catch a squirrel?' asked Kamla.

'No, they are too quick. But I caught a snake once. I caught it by its tail and dropped it in the old well. That well is full of snakes. Whenever we catch one, instead of killing it, we drop it into the well! They can't get out.'

Kamla shuddered at the thought of all those snakes swimming and wriggling about at the bottom of the deep well. She wasn't sure that she wanted to return to the well with him. But she forgot about the snakes when they reached the canal.

It was a small canal, about ten metres wide, and only waist-deep in the middle, but it was very muddy at the bottom. She had never seen such a muddy stream in her life.

'Would you like to get in?' asked Romi.

'No,' said Kamla. 'You get in.'

Romi was only too ready to show off his tricks in the water. His toes took a firm hold on the grassy bank, the muscles of his calves tensed, and he dived into the water with a loud splash, landing rather awkwardly on his belly. It was a poor dive, but Kamla was impressed.

Romi swam across to the opposite bank and then back again.

When he climbed out of the water, he was covered with mud. It made him look quite fierce. 'Come on in,' he invited. 'It's not deep.'

'It's dirty,' said Kamla, but felt tempted all the same.

'It's only mud,' urged Romi. 'There's nothing wrong with mud. Camels like mud. Buffaloes love mud.'

'I'm not a camel—or a buffalo.'

'All right. You don't have to go right in, just walk along the sides of the channel.'

After a moment's hesitation, Kamla slipped her feet out of her slippers, and crept cautiously down the slope till her feet were in the water. She went no further, but even so, some of the muddy water splashed on to her clean, white skirt. What would she tell Grandmother? Her feet sank into the soft mud and she gave a little squeal as the water reached her knees. It was with some difficulty that she got each foot out of the sticky mud.

Romi took her by the hand, and they went stumbling along the side of the channel while little fish swam in and out of their legs, and a heron, one foot raised, waited until they had passed before snapping a fish out of the water. The little fish glistened in the sun before it disappeared down the heron's throat.

Romi gave a sudden exclamation and came to a stop. Kamla held on to him for support.

'What is it?' she asked, a little nervously.

'It's a tortoise,' said Romi. 'Can you see it?'

He pointed to the bank of the canal, and there, lying quite still, was a small tortoise. Romi scrambled up the bank and, before Kamla could stop him, had picked up the tortoise. As soon as he touched it, the animal's head and legs disappeared into its shell. Romi turned it over, but from behind the breastplate only the head and a spiky tail were visible.

'Look!' exclaimed Kamla, pointing to the ground where the tortoise had been lying. 'What's in that hole?'

They peered into the hole. It was about half a metre deep, and at the bottom were five or six white eggs, a little smaller than a hen's eggs.

'Put the tortoise back,' said Kamla. 'It was sitting on its eggs.'

Romi shrugged and dropped the tortoise back on its hole. It peeped out from behind its shell, saw the children were still present, and retreated into its shell again.

'I must go,' said Kamla. 'It's getting late. Grandmother will wonder where I have gone.'

They walked back to the mango tree, and washed their hands and feet in the cool, clear water from the well, but only after Romi had assured Kamla that there weren't any snakes in this well—he had been talking about an old disused well on the far side of the village. Kamla told Romi she would take him to her house one day, but it would have to be next year, or perhaps the year after, when she came to India again.

'Is it very far, where you are going?' asked Romi.

'Yes, England is across the seas. I have to go back to my parents. And my school is there, too. But I will take the plane from Delhi. Have you ever been to Delhi?'

'I have not been further than Jaipur,' said Romi. 'What is England like? Are there canals to swim in?'

'You can swim in the sea. Lots of people go swimming in the sea. But it's too cold most of the year. Where I live, there are shops and cinemas and places where you can eat anything you like. And people from all over the world come to live there. You can see red faces, brown faces, black faces, white faces!'

'I saw a red face once,' said Romi. 'He came to the village to take pictures. He took one of me sitting on the camel. He said he would send me the picture, but it never came.'

Kamla noticed the flute lying on the grass. 'Is it your flute?' she asked.

'Yes,' answered Romi. 'It is an old flute. But the old ones are best. I found it lying in a field last year. Perhaps it was Lord Krishna's! He was always playing the flute.'

'And who taught you to play it?'

'Nobody. I learnt by myself. Shall I play it for you?'

Kamla nodded, and they sat down on the grass, leaning against the trunk of the mango tree, and Romi put the flute to his lips and began to play.

It was a slow, sweet tune, a little sad, a little happy, and the notes were taken up by the breeze and carried across the fields.

There was no one to hear the music except the birds and the camel and Kamla. Whether the camel liked it or not, we shall never know; it just kept going round and round the well, drawing up water for the fields. And whether the birds liked it or not, we cannot say, although it is true that they were all suddenly silent when Romi began to play. But Kamla was charmed by the music, and she watched Romi while he played, and the boy smiled at her with his eyes and ran his fingers along the flute. When he stopped playing, everything was still, everything silent, except for the soft wind sighing in the wheat and the gurgle of water coming up from the well.

Kamla stood up to leave.

'When will you come again?' asked Romi.

'I will try to come next year,' said Kamla.

'That is a long time. By then you will be quite old. You may not want to come.'

'I will come,' repeated Kamla.

'Promise?'

'Promise.'

Romi put the flute in her hands and said, 'You keep it. I can get another one.'

'But I don't know how to play it,' protested Kamla.

'It will play by itself,' replied Romi.

She took the flute and put it to her lips and blew on it, producing a squeaky little note that startled a lone parrot out of the mango tree. Romi laughed, and while he was laughing, Kamla turned and ran down the path through the fields. And when she had gone some distance, she turned and waved to Romi with the flute. He stood near the well and waved back at her.

Cupping his hands to his mouth, he shouted across the fields, 'Don't forget to come next year!'

And Kamla called back, 'I won't forget.' But her voice was faint, and the breeze blew the words away and Romi did not hear them.

Was England home? wondered Kamla. Or was this Indian city home? Or was her true home in that other India, across the busy Trunk Road? Perhaps she would find out one day.

Romi watched her until she was just a speck in the distance, and then he turned and shouted at the camel, telling it to move faster. But the camel did not even glance at him; it just carried on as before, as India has carried on for thousands of years, round and round and round the well, while the water gurgled and splashed over the smooth stones.

The Hidden Pool

It was going to rain. I could see the rain moving across the foothills, and I could smell it in the breeze. But instead of turning homewards, I pushed my way through the leaves and brambles that grew across the forest path. I had heard the sound of running water at the bottom of the hill, and I was determined to find this hidden stream.

I had to slide down a rock face into a small ravine, and there I found the stream running over a bed of shingle. I removed my shoes and started walking upstream. A large, glossy, black bird with a curved, red beak hooted at me as I passed and a paradise flycatcher—this one I couldn't fail to recognize, with its long, fan-like tail beating the air—swooped across the stream. Water trickled down from the hillside, from amongst ferns and grasses and wild flowers; and the hills, rising steeply on either side, kept the ravine in shadow. The rocks were smooth, almost soft, and some of them were grey and some yellow. A small waterfall came down the rocks and formed a deep, round pool of apple-green water.

When I saw the pool, I turned and ran home. I wanted to tell Anil and Kamal about it. It began to rain, but I didn't stop to take shelter, I ran all the way home—through the sal forest, across the dry riverbed, through the outskirts of the town.

Though Anil usually chose the adventures we were to have, the pool was my own discovery, and I was proud of it.

'We'll call it Laurie's Pool,' declared Kamal. 'And remember, it's a secret pool. No one else must know of it.'

I think it was the pool that brought us together more than anything else.

Kamal was the best swimmer. He dived off rocks and went gliding about under the water like a long, golden fish. Anil had strong legs and arms, and he threshed about with much vigour but little skill. I could dive off a rock too, but I usually landed on my stomach.

There were slim, silver fish in the stream. At first, we tried catching them with a line, but they soon learnt the art of taking the bait without being caught on the hook. Next, we tried a bedsheet (Anil had removed one from his mother's laundry) which we stretched across one end of the stream, but the fish wouldn't come anywhere near it. Eventually Anil, without telling us, procured a stick of gunpowder. And Kamal and I were startled out of an afternoon siesta by a flash across the water and a deafening explosion. Half the hillside tumbled into the pool, and Anil along with it. We got him out, along with a large supply of stunned fish which were too small for eating. Anil, however, didn't want all his work to go waste. So he roasted the fish over a fire and ate them himself.

The effects of the explosion gave Anil another idea, which was to enlarge our pool by building a dam across one end. This he accomplished with our combined labour. But he had chosen a week when there had been heavy rain in the hills, and we had barely finished making the dam when a torrent of water came rushing down the bed of the stream, bursting our earthworks and flooding the ravine. Our clothes were carried away by the current, and we had to wait until it was night before creeping into town through the darkest alleyways. Anil was spotted at a street corner, but he posed as a naked sadhu and began calling for alms, and finally slipped in through the back door of his house without being recognized. I had to lend Kamal some of my clothes, and these, made him look odd and gangly because I was of a much smaller size.

Our other activities at the pool included wrestling and buffalo riding.

We wrestled on a strip of sand that ran beside the stream. Anil had often attended the wrestling akhara and was something of an expert. Kamal and I usually combined against him and after five or ten minutes of furious, unscientific struggle, we usually succeeded in flattening Anil into the sand; Kamal would sit on his head, and I would sit on his legs until he admitted defeat. There was no fun in taking him on singly, because he knew too many tricks for us.

We rode on a couple of buffaloes that sometimes came to drink and wallow in the more muddy parts of the stream. Buffaloes are fine, sluggish creatures, always in search of a soft, slushy resting place. We would climb on their backs, kick, yell and urge them forward, but on no occasion did we succeed on getting them to carry us anywhere. If they got tired of our antics, they would merely roll over on their backs, taking us with them into a bed of muddy water.

Not that it mattered how muddy we got, because we had only to dive into the pool to get rid of it all. The buffaloes couldn't get to the pool because of its narrow outlet and the slippery rocks.

If it was possible for Anil and me to slip out of our homes at night, we would come to the pool for a swim by moonlight. We would often find Kamal there before us. He wasn't afraid of the dark or the surrounding forest, where there were panthers and jungle cats. We bathed silently at nights, because the stillness of the surrounding jungle seemed to discourage high spirits; but sometimes Kamal would sing—he had a clear, ringing voice—and we would float the red, long-fingered poinsettias downstream.

The pool was to be our principal meeting place during the coming months. It was not that we couldn't meet in town. But the pool was secret, known only to us, and it gave us a feeling of conspiracy and adventure to meet there after school. It was at the pool that we made our plans, it was at the pool that we first spoke of the glacier; but several weeks and few other exploits were to pass before that particular dream materialized.

The Leopard

I first saw the leopard when I was crossing the small stream at the bottom of the hill.

The ravine was so deep that for most of the day it remained in shadow. This encouraged many birds and animals to emerge from cover during the daylight hours. Few people ever passed that way—only milkmen and charcoal burners from the surrounding villages. As a result, the ravine had become a little haven for wildlife, one of the few natural sanctuaries left near Mussoorie.

Below my cottage was a forest of oak and maple and Himalayan rhododendron. A narrow path twisted its way down through the trees, over an open ridge where red sorrel grew wild, and then steeply down through a tangle of wild raspberries, creeping vines and slender bamboo. At the bottom of the hill the path led on to a grassy verge, surrounded by wild dog roses. (It is surprising how closely the flora of the lower Himalayas, between five thousand and eight thousand feet, resembles that of the English countryside.)

The stream ran close by the verge, tumbling over smooth pebbles, over rocks worn yellow with age, on its way to the plains and to the little Song River and finally to the sacred Ganga.

When I first discovered the stream, it was early April and the wild roses were flowering—small, white blossoms lying in clusters. I walked down to the stream almost every day after two or three hours of writing. I had lived in cities too long and had returned to the hills to renew myself, both physically and mentally. Once you have lived with mountains for any length of time you belong to them, and must return again and again.

Nearly every morning, and sometimes during the day, I heard the cry of the barking deer. And in the evening, walking through the forest, I disturbed parties of pheasants. The birds went gliding down the ravine on open, motionless wings. I saw pine martens and a handsome red fox, and I recognized the footprints of a bear.

As I had not come to take anything from the forest, the birds and animals soon grew accustomed to my presence. Possibly they recognized my footsteps. After some time, my approach did not disturb them.

The langoors in the oak and rhododendron trees, who would at first go leaping through the branches on seeing me, now watched me with some curiosity as they munched the tender, green shoots of the oak. The young ones scuffled and wrestled like boys while their parents groomed each other's coats, stretching themselves out on the sunlit hillside.

But one evening, as I passed, I heard them chattering in the trees, and I knew I was not the cause of their excitement. As I crossed the stream and began climbing the hill, the grunting and chattering increased, as though the langoors were trying to warn me of some hidden danger. A shower of pebbles came rattling down the steep hillside, and I looked up to see a sinewy, orange-gold leopard poised on a rock about twenty feet above.

He was not looking towards me but had his head thrust attentively forward, in the direction of the ravine. Yet he must have sensed my presence, because he slowly turned his head and looked down at me.

He seemed a little puzzled at my being there; and when, to give myself courage, I clapped my hands sharply, the leopard sprang away into the thickets, making absolutely no sound as he melted into the shadows.

I had disturbed the animal in his quest for food. But a little after I heard the quickening cry of a barking deer as it fled through the forest. The hunt was still on.

The leopard, like other members of the cat family, is nearing extinction in India, and I was surprised to find one so close to Mussoorie. Probably the deforestation that had been taking place in the surrounding hills had driven the deer into this green valley; and the leopard, naturally, had followed.

It was some weeks before I saw the leopard again, although I was often made aware of his presence. A dry, rasping cough sometimes gave him away. At times I felt almost certain that I was being followed.

Once, when I was late getting home, and the brief twilight gave way to a dark, moonless night, I was startled by a family of porcupines running about in a clearing. I looked around nervously and saw two bright eyes staring at me from a thicket. I stood still, my heart banging away against my ribs. Then the eyes danced away and I realized that they were only fireflies.

In May and June, when the hills were brown and dry, it was always cool and green near the stream, where ferns and maidenhair and long grasses continued to thrive.

Downstream, I found a small pool where I could bathe, and a cave with water dripping from the roof, the water spangled gold and silver in the shafts of sunlight that pushed through the slits in the cave roof.

The hill station's summer visitors had not discovered this haven of wild and green things. I was beginning to feel that the place belonged to me, dominion was mine.

The stream had at least one other regular visitor, a spotted forktail, and though she did not fly away at my approach, she became restless if I stayed too long, and then she would move from boulder to boulder uttering a long, complaining cry.

I spent an afternoon trying to discover the bird's nest, which I was certain contained young ones, because I had seen the forktail carrying grub in her bill. The problem was that when the bird flew upstream, I had difficulty in following her rapidly enough as the rocks were sharp and slippery.

Eventually I decorated myself with bracken fronds and, after slowly making my way upstream, hid myself in the hollow stump of a tree at a spot where the forktail often disappeared. I had no intention of robbing the bird. I was simply curious to see its home. By crouching down, I was able to command a view of a small stretch of the stream and the side of the ravine; but I had done little to deceive the forktail, who continued to object strongly to my presence so near her home.

I summoned up my reserves of patience and sat perfectly still for about ten minutes. The forktail quietened down. Out of sight, out of mind. But where had she gone? Probably into the walls of the ravine where, I felt sure, she was guarding her nest.

I decided to take her by surprise and stood up suddenly, in time to see not the forktail on her doorstep but the leopard bounding away with a grunt of surprise! Two urgent springs, and he had crossed the stream and plunged into the forest.

I was as astonished as the leopard, and forgot all about the forktail and her nest. Had the leopard been following me again? I decided against this possibility. Only man-eaters follow humans and, as far as I knew, there had never been a man-eater in the vicinity of Mussoorie.

During the monsoon the stream became a rushing torrent; bushes and small trees were swept away, and the friendly murmur of the water became a threatening boom. I did not visit the place too often as there were leeches in the long grass.

One day I found the remains of a barking deer, which had only been partly eaten. I wondered why the leopard had not hidden the rest of his meal, and decided that he must have been disturbed while eating.

Then, climbing the hill, I met a party of hunters resting beneath the oaks. They asked me if I had seen a leopard. I replied that I had not. They said they knew there was a leopard in the forest.

Leopard skins, they told me, were selling in Delhi at over a thousand rupees each. Of course there was a ban on the export of skins, but they gave me to understand that there were ways and means . . . I thanked them for their information and walked on, feeling uneasy and disturbed.

The hunters had seen the carcass of the deer, and they had seen the leopard's pug marks, and they kept returning to the forest. Almost every evening I heard their guns banging away; for they were ready to fire at almost anything.

'There's a leopard about,' they warned me. 'You should carry a gun.'

'I don't have one,' I said.

There were fewer birds to be seen, and even the langoors had moved on. The red fox did not show itself; and the pine martens, who had become quite bold, now dashed into hiding at my approach. The smell of one human is like the smell of any other.

And then the rains were over and it was October. I could lie in the sun, on sweet-smelling grass, and gaze up through a pattern of oak leaves into a blinding blue heaven. And I would praise God for leaves and grass and the smell of things—the smell of mint and bruised clover—and the touch of things—the touch of grass and air and sky, the touch of the sky's blueness.

I thought no more of the men. My attitude towards them was similar to that of the denizens of the forest. These were men, unpredictable, and to be avoided if possible.

On the other side of the ravine rose Pari Tibba, hill of the fairies; a bleak, scrub-covered hill where no one lived.

It was said that in the previous century Englishmen had tried building their houses on the hill, but the area had always attracted lightning, due to either the hill's location or due to its mineral deposits. After several houses had been struck by lightning, the settlers moved on to the next hill, where the town now stands.

To the hillmen it is Pari Tibba, haunted by the spirits of a pair of ill-fated lovers who perished there in a storm; to others it is known as Burnt Hill, because of its scarred and stunted trees.

One day, after crossing the stream, I climbed Pari Tibba—a stiff undertaking, because there was no path to the top and I had to scramble up a precipitous rock face with the help of rocks and roots that were apt to come loose in my groping hand.

But at the top was a plateau with a few pine trees, their upper branches catching the wind and humming softly. There I found the ruins of what must have been the houses of the first settlers—just a few piles of rubble, now overgrown with weeds, sorrel, dandelions and nettles.

As I walked though the roofless ruins, I was struck by the silence that surrounded me, the absence of birds and animals, and the sense of complete desolation.

The silence was so absolute that it seemed to be ringing in my ears. But there was something else of which I was becoming increasingly aware: the strong feline odour of one of the cat family. I paused and looked about. I was alone. There was no movement of dry leaf or loose stone.

The ruins were for the most part open to the sky. Their rotting rafters had collapsed, jamming together to form a low passage like the entrance to a mine; and this dark cavern seemed to lead down into the ground. The smell was stronger when I approached this spot, so I stopped again and waited there, wondering if I had discovered the lair of the leopard, wondering if the animal was now at rest after a night's hunt.

Perhaps he was crouching there in the dark, watching me, recognizing me, knowing me as the man who walked alone in the forest without a weapon.

I like to think that he was there, that he knew me, and that he acknowledged my visit in the friendliest way: by ignoring me altogether.

Perhaps I had made him confident—too confident, too careless, too trusting of the human in his midst. I did not venture any further; I was not out of my mind. I did not seek physical contact, or even another glimpse of that beautiful, sinewy body, springing from rock to rock. It was his trust I wanted, and I think he gave it to me.

But did the leopard, trusting one man, make the mistake of bestowing his trust on others? Did I, by casting out all fear—my own fear, and the leopard's protective fear—leave him defenceless?

Because the next day, coming up the path from the stream, shouting and beating drums, were the hunters. They had a long bamboo pole across their shoulders, and slung from the pole, feet up, head down, was the lifeless body of the leopard, shot in the neck and in the head.

'We told you there was a leopard!' they shouted, in great good humour. 'Isn't he a fine specimen?'

'Yes,' I said. 'He was a beautiful leopard.'

I walked home through the silent forest. It was very silent, almost as though the birds and animals knew that their trust had been violated.

I remembered the lines of a poem by D.H. Lawrence; and, as I climbed the steep and lonely path to my home, the words beat out their rhythm in my mind: 'There was room in the world for a mountain lion and me.'

Would Astley Return?

The house was called Undercliff because that's where it stood—under a cliff. The man who went away—the owner of the house—was Robert Astley. And the man who stayed behind—the old family retainer—was Prem Bahadur.

Astley had been gone many years. He was still a bachelor in his late thirties when he'd suddenly decided that he wanted adventure, romance and faraway places. And he'd given the keys of the house to Prem Bahadur—who'd served the family for thirty years—and had set off on his travels.

Someone saw him in Sri Lanka. He'd been heard of in Burma around the ruby mines at Mogok. Then he turned up in Java seeking a passage through the Sunda Straits. After that the trail petered out. Years passed. The house in the hill station remained empty.

But Prem Bahadur was still there, living in an outhouse.

Every day he opened up Undercliff, dusted the furniture in all the rooms, made sure that the bedsheets and pillowcases were clean and set out Astley's dressing gown and slippers.

In the old days, whenever Astley had come home after a journey or a long tramp in the hills, he had liked to bathe and change into his gown and slippers, no matter what the hour. Prem Bahadur still kept them ready. He was convinced that Robert would return one day.

Astley himself had said so.

'Keep everything ready for me, Prem, old chap. I may be back after a year, or two years, or even longer, but I'll be back, I promise you. On the first of every month I want you to go to my lawyer, Mr Kapoor. He'll give you your salary and any money that's needed for the rates and repairs. I want you to keep the house tip-top!'

'Will you bring back a wife, sahib?'

'Lord, no! Whatever put that idea in your head?'

'I thought, perhaps—because you wanted the house kept ready . . .'

'Ready for me, Prem. I don't want to come home and find the old place falling down.'

And so Prem had taken care of the house—although there was no news from Astley. What had happened to him? The mystery provided a talking point whenever local people met on the Mall. And in the bazaar the shopkeepers missed Astley because he had been a man who spent freely.

His relatives still believed him to be alive. Only a few months back a brother had turned up—a brother who had a farm in Canada and could not stay in India for long. He had deposited a further sum with the lawyer and told Prem to carry on as before. The salary provided Prem with his few needs. Moreover, he was convinced that Robert would return.

Another man might have neglected the house and grounds, but not Prem Bahadur. He had a genuine regard for the absent owner. Prem was much older—now almost sixty and none too strong, suffering from pleurisy and other chest troubles—but he remembered Robert as both a boy and a young man. They had been together on numerous hunting and fishing trips in the mountains. They had slept out under the stars, bathed in icy mountain streams together, and eaten from the same cooking pot. Once, when crossing a small river, they had been swept downstream by a flash flood, a wall of water that came thundering down the gorges without any warning during the rainy season. Together they had struggled back to safety. Back in the hill station, Astley told everyone that Prem had saved his life while Prem was equally insistent that he owed his life to Robert.

This year the monsoon had begun early and ended late. It dragged on through most of September and Prem Bahadur's cough grew worse and his breathing more difficult.

He lay on his charpoy on the veranda, staring out at the garden, which was beginning to get out of hand, a tangle of dahlias, snake lilies and convolvulus. The sun finally came out. The wind shifted from the south-west to the north-west and swept the clouds away.

Prem Bahadur had shifted his charpoy into the garden and was lying in the sun, puffing at his small hookah, when he saw Robert Astley at the gate.

Prem tried to get up but his legs would not oblige him. The hookah slipped from his hand.

Astley came walking down the garden path and stopped in front of the old retainer, smiling down at him. He did not look a day older than when Prem Bahadur had last seen him.

'So you have come at last,' said Prem.

'I told you I'd return.'

'It has been many years. But you have not changed.'

'Nor have you, old chap.'

'I have grown old and sick and feeble.'

'You'll be fine now. That's why I've come.'

'I'll open the house,' said Prem and this time he found himself getting up quite easily.

'It isn't necessary,' answered Astley.

'But all is ready for you!'

'I know. I have heard of how well you have looked after everything. Come then, let's take a last look around. We cannot stay, you know.'

Prem was a little mystified but he opened the front door and took Robert through the drawing room and up the stairs to the bedroom. Robert noticed the dressing gown and the slippers and he placed his hand gently on the old man's shoulder.

When they returned downstairs and emerged into the sunlight Prem was surprised to see himself—or rather his skinny body—stretched out on the charpoy. The hookah was on the ground, where it had fallen.

Prem looked at Astley in bewilderment.

'But who is that lying there?'

'It was you. Only the husk now, the empty shell. This is the real you, standing here beside me.'

'You came for me?'

'I couldn't come until you were ready. As for me, I left my

shell a long time ago. But you were determined to hang on, keeping this house together. Are you ready now?'

'And the house?'

'Others will live in it. But come, it's time to go fishing . . .'

Astley took Prem by the arm, and they walked through the dappled sunlight under the deodars and finally left that place forever.

The Story of Madhu

I met little Madhu several years ago, when I lived alone in an obscure town near the Himalayan foothills. I was in my late twenties then, and my outlook on life was still quite romantic; the cynicism that was to come with the thirties had not yet set in.

I preferred the solitude of the small district town to the kind of social life I might have found in the cities; and in my books, my writing and the surrounding hills, there was enough for my pleasure and occupation.

On summer mornings I would often sit beneath an old mango tree, with a notebook or a sketch pad on my knees. The house which I had rented (for a very nominal sum) stood on the outskirts of the town, and a large tank and a few poor houses could be seen from the garden wall. A narrow public pathway passed under the low wall.

One morning, while I sat beneath the mango tree, I saw a young girl of about nine, wearing torn clothes, darting about on the pathway and along the high banks of the tank.

Sometimes she stopped to look at me; and, when I showed that I had noticed her, she felt encouraged and gave me a shy, fleeting smile. The next day I discovered her leaning over the garden wall, following my actions as I paced up and down on the grass.

In a few days an acquaintance had been formed. I began to take the girl's presence for granted, and even to look for her, and she, in turn, would linger about on the pathway until she saw me come out of the house.

One day, as she passed the gate, I called her to me.

'What is your name?' I asked. 'And where do you live?'

'Madhu,' she replied, brushing back her long, untidy black hair and smiling at me from large, black eyes. She pointed across the road: 'I live with my grandmother.'

'Is she very old?' I asked.

Madhu nodded confidingly and whispered: 'A hundred years . . .'

'We will never be that old,' I said. Madhu was very slight and frail, like a flower growing in a rock, vulnerable to wind and rain.

I discovered later that the old lady was not her grandmother but a childless woman who had found the baby girl on the banks of the tank. Madhu's real parentage was unknown, but the wizened old woman had, out of compassion, brought up the child as her own.

The gate once entered, Madhu included my garden in her circle of activities. She was there every morning, chasing butterflies, stalking squirrels, her voice brimming with laughter, her slight figure flitting about between the trees.

Sometimes, but not often, I gave her a toy or a new dress; and one day she put aside her shyness and brought me a present of a nosegay, made up of marigolds and wild blue cotton flowers.

'For you,' she said, and put the flowers in my lap.

'They are very beautiful,' I said, picking out the brightest marigold and putting it in her hair. 'But they are not as beautiful as you.'

More than a year passed before I began to take more than a mildly patronizing interest in Madhu.

It occurred to me after some time that she should be taught to read and write, and I asked a local teacher to give her lessons in the garden for an hour every day. Madhu clapped her hands with pleasure at the prospect of what was to be for her a fascinating new game.

In a few weeks Madhu was surprising us with her capacity for absorbing knowledge. She always came to me to repeat the lessons of the day and pestered me with questions on a variety of subjects. How big was the world? And were the stars really like our world? Or were they the sons and daughters of the sun and the moon?

My interest in Madhu deepened, and my life, so empty till then, became imbued with a new purpose. As she sat on the grass beside me, reading aloud, or listening to me with a look of complete trust and belief, all the love that had been lying dormant in me during my years of self-exile surfaced in a sudden surge of tenderness.

Three years glided away imperceptibly, and at the age of thirteen Madhu was on the verge of blossoming into a woman. I began to feel a certain responsibility towards her.

It was dangerous, I knew, to allow a child so pretty to live almost alone and unprotected, and to run unrestrained about the grounds. And in a censorious society she would be made to suffer if she spent too much time in my company.

Madhu could see no need for any separation but I decided to send her to a mission school in the next district, where I could visit her from time to time.

'But why?' asked Madhu. 'I can learn more from you and from the teacher who comes. I am so happy here.'

'You will meet other girls and make many friends,' I told her. 'I will come to see you. And, when you come home, we will be even happier. It is good that you should go.'

It was the middle of June, a hot and oppressive month in the Siwaliks. Madhu had expressed her readiness to go to school. When, one evening, I did not see her as usual in the garden, I thought nothing of it; but the next day I was informed that she had fever and could not leave the house.

Illness was something Madhu had not known before, and for this reason I felt afraid. I hurried down the path which led to the old woman's cottage. It seemed strange that I had never once entered it during my long friendship with Madhu.

It was a humble mud hut, the ceiling just high enough to enable me to stand upright, the room dark but clean. Madhu was lying on a string cot, exhausted by fever, her eyes closed, her long hair unkempt, one small hand hanging over the side.

It struck me then how little, during all this time, I had thought of her physical comforts. There was no chair in the room. I knelt down and took her hand in mine. I knew, from the fierce heat of her body that she was seriously ill.

She recognized my touch, and a smile passed across her face before she opened her eyes. She held on to my hand, then laid it across her cheek.

I looked round the little room in which she had grown up. It had scarcely an article of furniture apart from two string cots, on one of which the old woman sat and watched us, her white, wizened head nodding like a puppet's.

In a corner lay Madhu's little treasures. I recognized among them the presents which, during the past four years, I had given her. She had kept everything. On her dark arm she still wore a small piece of ribbon which I had playfully tied there about a year ago. She had given her heart, even before she was conscious of possessing one, to a stranger unworthy of the gift.

As the evening drew on, a gust of wind blew open the door of the dark room, and a gleam of sunshine streamed in, lighting up a portion of the wall. It was the time when every evening she would join me under the mango tree. She had been quiet for almost an hour, and now a slight pressure of her hand drew my eyes back to her face.

'What will we do now?' she said. 'When will you send me to school?'

'Not for a long time. First you must get well and strong. That is all that matters.'

She didn't seem to hear me. I think she knew she was dying, but she did not resent it happening.

'Who will read to you under the tree?' she went on. 'Who will look after you?' she asked, with the solicitude of a grown woman.

'You will, Madhu. You are grown up now. There will be no one else to look after me.'

The old woman was standing at my shoulder. A hundred years old—and little Madhu was slipping away. The woman took Madhu's hand from mine, and laid it gently down. I sat by the cot a little longer, and then I rose to go, all the loneliness in the world pressing upon my heart.

Here Comes Mr Oliver

Apart from being our Scoutmaster, Mr Oliver was also our maths teacher, a subject in which I some difficulty in obtaining pass marks. Sometimes I scraped through, usually I got something like 20 or 30 out of 100.

'Failed again, Bond,' Mr Oliver would say. 'What will you do when you grow up?'

'Become a Scoutmaster, sir.'

'Scoutmasters don't get paid. It's an honorary job. But you could become a cook. That would suit you.' He hadn't forgotten our Scout camp, when I had cooked for the camp.

If Mr Oliver was in a good mood, he'd give me grace marks, passing me by a mark or two. He wasn't a hard man, but he seldom smiled. He was very dark, thin, stooped (from a distance he looked like a question mark), and balding. He was about forty, still a bachelor, and it was said that he had been unlucky in love—that the girl he was going to marry had jilted him at the last moment, had run away with a sailor while he was waiting at the church, ready for the wedding ceremony. No wonder he always had such a sorrowful look.

Mr Oliver did have one inseparable companion—a Dachshund, a snappy little 'sausage' of a dog, who looked upon the human race and especially small boys with a certain disdain and hostility. We called him Hitler. He was impervious to overtures of friendship, and if you tried to pat or stroke him, he would do his best to bite your fingers—or your shin or ankle. However, he was devoted to Mr Oliver and followed him everywhere, except into the classroom; this our headmaster would not allow.

You remember the old nursery rhyme:

> Mary had a little lamb,
>
> Its fleece was white as snow,
>
> And everywhere that Mary went
>
> That lamb was sure to go.

Well, we made up our own version of the rhyme, and I must confess to having a hand in its composition. It went like this:

> Olly had a little dog,
>
> 'Twas never out of sight,
>
> And everyone that Olly met
>
> The dog was sure to bite!

It followed him about the school grounds. It followed him when he took a walk through the pines, to the Brockhurst tennis courts. It followed him into town and home again. Mr Oliver had no other friend, no other companion. The dog slept at the foot of Mr Oliver's bed. It did not sit at the breakfast table, but it had buttered toast for breakfast and soup and crackers for dinner. Mr Oliver had to take his lunch in the dining hall with the staff and boys, but he had an arrangement with one of the bearers whereby a plate of dal, rice and chapattis made its way to Mr Oliver's quarters and to his well-fed pet.

And then tragedy struck.

Mr Oliver and Hitler were returning to school after their evening walk through the pines. It was dusk, and the light was fading fast. Out of the shadows of the trees emerged a lean and hungry panther. It pounced on the hapless dog, flung it across the road, seized it between its powerful jaws and made off with its victim into the darkness of the forest.

Mr Oliver, untouched, was frozen into immobility for at least a minute. Then he began calling for help. Some bystanders who had witnessed the incident began shouting, too. Mr Oliver ran into the forest, but there was no sign of dog or panther.

Mr Oliver appeared to be a broken man. He went about his duties with a poker face, but we could all tell that he was grieving for his lost companion. In the classroom he was listless, indifferent to whether or not we followed his calculations on the blackboard. In times of personal loss, the Highest Common Factor made no sense.

Mr Oliver did not go any longer on his evening walks. He stayed in his room, playing cards with himself. He toyed with his food, pushing most of it aside; there were no chapattis to send home.

'Olly needs another pet,' said Bimal, wise in the ways of adults.

'Or a wife,' added Tata, who thought on those lines.

'He's too old. Over forty.'

'A pet is best,' I said. 'What about a parrot?'

'You can't take a parrot for a walk,' Bimal disagreed. 'Olly wants someone to walk beside him.'

'A cat, maybe.'

'Hitler hated cats. A cat would be an insult to Hitler's memory.'

'He needs another Dachshund. But there aren't any around here.'

'Any dog will do. We'll ask Chippu to get us a pup.'

Chippu ran the tuck shop. He lived in the Chotta Shimla bazaar, and occasionally we would ask him to bring us tops or marbles or comics or little things that we couldn't get in school. Five of us Boy Scouts contributed a rupee each, and we gave Chippu the money and asked him to get us a pup. 'A good breed,' we told him. 'Not a mongrel.'

The next evening Chippu turned up with a pup that seemed to be a combination of at least five different breeds—all good ones, no doubt. One ear lay flat, the other stood upright. It was spotted like a Dalmatian, but it had the legs of a Spaniel and the tail of a Pomeranian. It was quite fluffy and playful, and the tail wagged a lot, which was more than Hitler's ever did.

'It's quite pretty,' said Tata. 'Must be a female.'

'He may not want a female,' argued Bimal.

'Let's give it a try,' I suggested.

During our play hour, before the bell rang for supper, we left the pup on the steps outside Mr Oliver's front door. Then we knocked, and sped into the hibiscus bushes that lined the pathway.

Mr Oliver opened the door. He looked down at the pup with an expressionless face. The pup began to paw at Mr Oliver's shoes, loosening one of his laces in the process.

'Away with you!' muttered Mr Oliver. 'Buzz off!' And he pushed the pup away, gently but firmly.

After a break of ten minutes we tried again, but the result was much the same. We now had a playful pup on our hands, and Chippu had gone home for the night. We would have to conceal it in the dormitory.

At first we hid the pup in Bimal's locker, but it began yapping and struggling to get out. Tata took it into the shower room, but it wouldn't stay there either. It began running around the dormitory, playing with socks, shoes, slippers, and anything else it could get hold of.

'Watch out!' hissed one of the boys. 'Here's Ma Fisher!'

Mrs Fisher, the headmaster's wife, was on her nightly rounds, checking to make sure we were all in bed and not up to some mischief.

I grabbed the pup and hid it under my blankets. It was quiet there, happy to nibble at my toes. When Ma Fisher had gone, I let the pup loose again, and for the rest of the night it had the freedom of the dormitory.

At the crack of dawn, before first light, Bimal and I sped out of the dormitory in our pyjamas, taking the pup with us. We banged hard on Mr Oliver's door, and kept knocking until we heard footsteps approaching. As soon as the door opened just a bit (for Mr Oliver, being a cautious man, did not open it all at once) we pushed the pup inside and ran for our lives.

Mr Oliver came to class as usual, but there was no pup with him. Three or four days passed, and still no sign of the pup. Had he passed it on to someone else, or simply let it wander off on its own?

'Here comes Olly!' called Bimal, from our vantage point near the school bell.

Mr Oliver was setting out for his evening walk. He was carrying a stout walnut-wood walking stick—to keep panthers at bay, no doubt. He looked neither left nor right, and if he noticed us watching him, he gave no sign of it. But then, scurrying behind him, came the pup! The creature of many good breeds was accompanying Mr Oliver on his walk. It had been well brushed and was wearing a bright, red collar. Like Mr Oliver it took no notice of us, but scampered along beside its new master.

Mr Oliver and the pup were soon inseparable companions, and my friends and I were quite pleased with ourselves. Mr Oliver gave absolutely no indication that he knew where the pup had come from, but when the end-of-term exams were over, and Bimal and I were sure we had failed our maths paper, we were surprised to find that we had passed after all—with grace marks!

'Good old Olly!' said Bimal. 'So he knew all the time.'

Tata, of course, did not need grace marks; he was a whiz at maths. But Bimal and I decided we would thank our teacher for his kindness.

'Nothing to thank me for,' said Mr Oliver brusquely. 'I've seen enough of you two in junior school. It's high time you went up to the senior school and God help you there!'

The Playing Fields of Shimla

It had been a lonely winter for a twelve-year-old boy.

I hadn't really got over my father's untimely death two years previously, nor had I as yet reconciled myself to my mother's marriage to the Punjabi gentleman who dealt in second-hand cars. The three-month winter break over, I was almost happy to return to my boarding school in Shimla—that elegant hill station once celebrated by Kipling and soon to lose its status as the summer capital of the Raj in India.

It wasn't as though I had many friends at school. I had always been a bit of a loner, shy and reserved, looking out only for my father's rare visits—on his brief leaves from RAF duties—and to my sharing his tent or air force encampment outside Delhi or Karachi. Those unsettled but happy days would not come again. I needed a friend but it was not easy to find one among a horde of rowdy, pea-shooting fourth formers, who carved their names on desks and stuck chewing gum on the class teacher's chair. Had I grown up with other children, I might have developed a taste for schoolboy anarchy; but, in sharing my father's loneliness after his separation from my mother, I had turned into a premature adult. The mixed nature of my reading—Dickens, Richmal Crompton, Tagore and Champion and Film Fun comics—probably reflected the confused state of my life. A book reader was rare even in those pre-electronic times. On rainy days most boys played cards or Monopoly, or listened to Artie Shaw on the wind-up gramophone in the common room.

After a month in the fourth form I began to notice a new boy, Omar, and then only because he was a quiet, almost taciturn person who took no part in the form's feverish attempts to imitate the Marx Brothers at the circus. Omar showed no resentment at the prevailing anarchy, nor did he make a move to participate in it. Once he caught me looking at him, and he smiled ruefully, tolerantly. Did I sense another adult in the class? Someone who was a little older than his years?

Even before we began talking to each other, Omar and I developed an understanding of sorts, and we'd nod almost respectfully to each other when we met in the classroom corridors or the environs of the dining hall or dormitory. We were not in the same house. The house system practised its own form of apartheid, whereby a member of, say, Curzon House was not expected to fraternize with someone belonging to Rivaz or Lefroy! Those public schools certainly knew how to clamp you into compartments. However, these barriers vanished when Omar and I found ourselves selected for the School Colts' hockey team—Omar as a full back, I as goalkeeper. I think a defensive position suited me by nature. In all modesty I have to say that I made a good goalkeeper, both at hockey and football. And fifty years on, I am still keeping goal. Then I did it between goalposts, now I do it off the field—protecting a family, protecting my independence as a writer . . .

The taciturn Omar now spoke to me occasionally, and we combined well on the field of play. A good understanding is needed between goalkeeper and full back. We were on the same wavelength. I anticipated his moves, he was familiar with mine. Years later, when I read Conrad's *The Secret Sharer*, I thought of Omar.

It wasn't until we were away from the confines of school, classroom and dining hall that our friendship flourished. The hockey team travelled to Sanawar on the next mountain range, where we were to play a couple of matches against our old rivals, the Lawrence Royal Military School. This had been my father's old school, but I did not know that in his time it had also been a military orphanage. Grandfather, who had been a private foot soldier—of the likes of Kipling's Mulvaney, Otheris and Learoyd—had joined the Scottish Rifles after leaving home at the age of seventeen. He had died while his children were still very young, but my father's more rounded education had enabled him to become an officer.

Omar and I were thrown together a good deal during the visit to Sanawar, and in our more leisurely moments, strolling undisturbed around a school where we were guests and not pupils, we exchanged life histories and other confidences. Omar, too, had lost his father—had I sensed that before?—shot in some tribal encounter at the Frontier, for he hailed from the lawless lands beyond Peshawar. A wealthy uncle was seeing to Omar's education.

The RAF was now seeing to mine.

We wandered into the school chapel, and there I found my father's name—A.A. Bond—on the school's roll of honour board: old boys who had lost their lives while serving during the two world wars.

'What did his initials stand for?' asked Omar.

'Aubrey Alexander.'

'Unusual name, like yours. Why did your parents call you Ruskin?'

'I am not sure. I think my father liked the works of John Ruskin, who wrote on serious subjects like art and architecture. I don't think anyone reads him now. They'll read me, though!' I had already started writing my first book. It was called *Nine Months* (the length of the school term, not a pregnancy!), and it described some of the happenings at school and lampooned a few of our teachers. I had filled three, slim exercise books with this premature literary project, and I allowed Omar to go through them. He must have been my first reader and critic. 'They're very interesting,' he said, 'but you'll get into trouble if someone finds them. Especially Mr Oliver.' And he read out an offending verse—

Olly, Olly, Olly, with his balls on a trolley,

And his arse all painted green!

I have to admit it wasn't great literature. I was better at hockey and football. I made some spectacular saves, and we won our matches against Sanawar. When we returned to Shimla, we were school heroes for a couple of days and lost some of our reticence; we were even a little more forthcoming with other boys. And then Mr Fisher, my housemaster, discovered my literary opus, *Nine Months*, under my mattress, and took it away and read it (as he told me later) from cover to cover. Corporal punishment then being in vogue, I was given six of the best with a springy malacca cane, and my manuscript was torn up and deposited in Fisher's wastepaper basket. All I had to show for my efforts were some purple welts on my bottom. These were proudly displayed to all who were interested, and I was a hero for another two days.

'Will you go away too when the British leave India?' Omar asked me one day.

'I don't think so,' I said. 'My stepfather is Indian.'

'Everyone is saying that our leaders and the British are going to divide the country. Shimla will be in India, Peshawar in Pakistan!'

'Oh, it won't happen,' I answered glibly. 'How can they cut up such a big country?' But even as we chatted about the possibility, Nehru and Jinnah and Mountbatten and all those who mattered were preparing their instruments for major surgery.

Before their decision impinged on our lives and everyone else's, we found a little freedom of our own—in an underground tunnel that we discovered below the third flat.

It was really part of an old, disused drainage system, and when Omar and I began exploring it, we had no idea just how far it extended. After crawling along on our bellies for some twenty feet, we found ourselves in complete darkness. Omar had brought along a small pencil torch, and with its help we continued writhing forward (moving backwards would have been quite impossible) until we saw a glimmer of light at the end of the tunnel. Dusty, musty, very scruffy, we emerged at last on to a grassy knoll, a little way outside the school boundary.

It's always a great thrill to escape beyond the boundaries that adults have devised. Here we were in unknown territory. To travel without passports—that would be the ultimate in freedom!

But more passports were on their way and more boundaries. Lord Mountbatten, Viceroy and Governor General-to-be, came for our Founder's Day and gave away the prizes. I had won a prize for something or the other, and mounted the rostrum to receive my book from this towering, handsome man in his pinstripe suit. Bishop Cotton's was then the premier school of India, often referred to as the 'Eton of the East'. Viceroys and Governors had graced its functions. Many of its boys had gone on to eminence in the civil services and the armed forces. There was one 'old boy' about whom however they maintained a stolid silence—General Dyer, who had ordered the massacre at Amritsar and destroyed the trust that had been building up between Britain and India.

Now Mountbatten spoke of the momentous events that were happening all around us—the war had just come to an end, the United Nations held out the promise of a world living in peace and harmony, and India, an equal partner with Britain, would be among the great nations . . .

A few weeks later, Bengal and Punjab provinces were bisected. Riots flared up across northern India, and there was a great exodus of people crossing the newly drawn frontiers between Pakistan and India. Homes were destroyed and thousands lost their lives.

The common room radio and the occasional newspaper kept us abreast of events, but in our tunnel, Omar and I felt immune from all that was happening, worlds away from all the pillage, murder and revenge. And outside the tunnel, on the pine knoll below the school, there was fresh, untrodden grass, sprinkled with clover and daisies, the only sounds the hammering of a woodpecker and the distant, insistent call of the Himalayan barbet. Who could touch us there?

'And when all the wars are done,' I said, 'a butterfly will still be beautiful.'

'Did you read that somewhere?'

'No, it just came into my head.'

'Already you're a writer.'

'No, I want to play hockey for India or football for Arsenal. Only winning teams!'

'You can't win forever. Better to be a writer.'

When the monsoon rains arrived, the tunnel was flooded, the drain choked with rubble. We were allowed out to the cinema to see Lawrence Olivier's *Hamlet*, a film that did nothing to raise our spirits on a wet and gloomy afternoon. But it was our last picture that year, because communal riots suddenly broke out in Shimla's Lower Bazaar, an area that was still much as Kipling had described it—'a man who knows his way there can defy all the police of India's summer capital'—and we were confined to school indefinitely.

One morning after chapel, the headmaster announced that the Muslim boys—those who had their homes in what was now Pakistan—would have to be evacuated, sent to their families across the border with an armed convoy.

The tunnel no longer provided an escape for us. The bazaar was out of bounds. The flooded playing field was deserted. Omar and I sat on a damp, wooden bench and talked about the future in vaguely hopeful terms; but we didn't solve any problems. Mountbatten and Nehru and Jinnah were doing all the solving.

It was soon time for Omar to leave along with some fifty other boys from Lahore, Pindi and Peshawar. The rest of us— Hindus, Christians, Parsis—helped them load their luggage into the waiting trucks. A couple of boys broke down and wept. So did our departing school captain, a Pathan who had been known for his stoic and unemotional demeanour. Omar waved cheerfully to me and I waved back. We had vowed to meet again someday.

The convoy got through safely enough. There was only one casualty—the school cook, who had strayed into an off-limits area in the foothill town of Kalka and been set upon by a mob. He was never seen again.

Towards the end of the school year, just as we were all getting ready to leave for the winter holidays, I received a letter from Omar. He told me something about his new school and how he missed my company and our games and our tunnel to freedom. I replied and gave him my home address, but I did not hear from him again. The land, though divided, was still a big one, and we were very small.

Some seventeen or eighteen years later I did get news of Omar, but in an entirely different context. India and Pakistan were at war and in a bombing raid over Ambala, not far from Shimla, a Pakistani plane was shot down. Its crew died in the crash. One of them, I learnt later, was Omar.

Did he, I wonder, get a glimpse of the playing fields we knew so well as boys?

Perhaps memories of our school days flooded back as he flew over the foothills. Perhaps he remembered the tunnel through which we were able to make our little escape to freedom.

But there are no tunnels in the sky.

The Prospect of Flowers

Fern Hill, The Oaks, Hunter's Lodge, The Parsonage, The Pines, Dumbarnie, Mackinnon's Hall and Windermere. These are the names of some of the old houses that still stand on the outskirts of one of the smaller Indian hill stations. Most of them have fallen into decay and ruin. They are very old, of course—built over a hundred years ago by Britishers who sought relief from the searing heat of the plains. Today's visitors to the hill stations prefer to live near the markets and cinemas, and many of the old houses, set amidst oak and maple and deodar, are inhabited by wild cats, bandicoots, owls, goats and the occasional charcoal burner or mule driver.

But among these neglected mansions stands a neat, whitewashed cottage called Mulberry Lodge. And in it, up to a short time ago, lived an elderly English spinster named Miss Mackenzie.

In years Miss Mackenzie was more than 'elderly', being well over eighty. But no one would have guessed it. She was clean, sprightly, and wore old-fashioned but well-preserved dresses. Once a week, she walked the two miles to town to buy butter and jam and soap and sometimes a small bottle of eau de cologne.

She had lived in the hill station since she had been a girl in her teens, and that had been before the First World War. Though she had never married, she had been in a few love affairs and was far from being the typical frustrated spinster of fiction. Her parents had been dead for thirty years; her brother and sister were also dead. She had no relatives in India, and she lived on a small pension of forty rupees a month and the gift parcels that were sent out to her from New Zealand by a friend of her youth.

Like other lonely, old people, Miss Mackenzie kept a pet—a large, black cat with bright, yellow eyes. In her small garden she grew dahlias, chrysanthemums, gladioli and a few rare orchids. She knew a great deal about plants and about wild flowers, trees, birds and insects. She had never made a serious study of these things, but having lived with them for so many years had developed an intimacy with all that grew and flourished around her.

She had few visitors. Occasionally, the padre from the local church called on her, and once a month the postman came with a letter from New Zealand or her pension papers. The milkman called every second day with a litre of milk for the lady and her cat. And sometimes she received a couple of eggs free, for the egg seller remembered a time when Miss Mackenzie, in her earlier prosperity, had bought eggs from him in large quantities. He was a sentimental man. He remembered her as a ravishing beauty in her twenties when he had gazed at her in round-eyed, nine-year-old wonder.

Now it was September and the rains were nearly over, and Miss Mackenzie's chrysanthemums were coming into their own. She hoped the coming winter wouldn't be too severe because she found it increasingly difficult to bear the cold.

One day, as she was pottering about in her garden, she saw a schoolboy plucking wild flowers on the slope about the cottage. 'Who's that?' she called. 'What are you up to, young man?'

The boy was alarmed and tried to dash up the hillside, but he slipped on pine needles and came slithering down the slope on to Miss Mackenzie's nasturtium bed.

When he found there was no escape, he gave a bright, disarming smile and said, 'Good morning, miss.'

He belonged to the local English-medium school and wore a bright red blazer and a red and black striped tie. Like most polite Indian schoolboys, he called every woman 'miss'.

'Good morning,' said Miss Mackenzie severely. 'Would you mind moving out of my flower bed?'

The boy stepped gingerly over the nasturtiums and looked up with dimpled cheeks and appealing eyes. It was impossible to be angry with him.

'You're trespassing,' said Miss Mackenzie.

'Yes, miss.'

'And you ought to be in school at this hour.'

'Yes, miss.'

'Then what are you doing here?'

'Picking flowers, miss.' And he held up a bunch of ferns and wild flowers.

'Oh.' Miss Mackenzie was disarmed. It was a long time since she had seen a boy taking an interest in flowers, and,

114

what was more, playing truant from school in order to gather them.

'Do you like flowers?' she asked.

'Yes, miss. I'm going to be a botan—a botantist?'

'You mean a botanist.'

'Yes, miss.'

'Well, that's unusual. Most boys at your age want to be pilots or soldiers or perhaps engineers. But you want to be a botanist. Well, well. There's still hope for the world, I see. And do you know the names of these flowers?'

'This is a *bukhilo* flower,' he said, showing her a small golden flower. 'That's a Pahari name. It means puja or prayer. The flower is offered during prayers. But I don't know what this is . . .'

He held out a pale, pink flower with a soft, heart-shaped leaf.

'It's a wild begonia,' said Miss Mackenzie. 'And that purple stuff is salvia, but it isn't wild. It's a plant that escaped from my garden. Don't you have any books on flowers?'

'No, miss.'

'All right, come in and I'll show you a book.'

She led the boy into a small front room, which was crowded with furniture and books and vases and jam jars, and offered him a chair. He sat awkwardly on its edge. The black cat immediately leapt on to his knees and settled down on them, purring loudly.

'What's your name?' asked Miss Mackenzie, as she rummaged through her books.

'Anil, miss.'

'And where do you live?'

'When school closes, I go to Delhi. My father has a business.'

'Oh, and what's that?'

'Bulbs, miss.'

'Flower bulbs?'

'No, electric bulbs.'

'Electric bulbs! You might send me a few, when you get home. Mine are always getting fused, and they're so expensive, like everything else these days. Ah, here we are!' She pulled a heavy volume down from the shelf and laid it on the table. '*Flora Himaliensis*, published in 1892, and probably the only copy in India. This is a very valuable book, Anil. No other naturalist has recorded so many wild Himalayan flowers. And let me tell you this, there are many flowers and plants which are still unknown to the fancy botanists who spend all their time with microscopes instead of in the mountains. But perhaps, *you'll* do something about that, one day.'

'Yes, miss.'

They went through the book together, and Miss Mackenzie pointed out many flowers that grew in and around hill stations, while the boy made notes of their names and seasons. She lit a stove, and put the kettle on for tea. And then the old English lady and the small Indian boy sat side by side over cups of hot, sweet tea, absorbed in a book on wild flowers.

'May I come again?' asked Anil, when he finally rose to go.

'If you like,' said Miss Mackenzie. 'But not during school hours. You mustn't miss your classes.'

After that, Anil visited Miss Mackenzie about once a week, and nearly always brought a wild flower for her to identify. She found herself looking forward to the boy's visits—and sometimes, when more than a week had passed and he didn't come, she was disappointed and lonely and would grumble at the black cat.

Anil reminded Miss Mackenzie of her brother, when the latter had been a boy. There was no physical resemblance. Andrew had been fair-haired and blue-eyed. But it was Anil's eagerness, his alert, bright look and the way he stood—legs apart, hands on hips, a picture of confidence—that reminded her of the boy who had shared her own youth in these same hills.

And why did Anil come to see her so often?

Partly because she knew about wild flowers and he really did want to become a botanist. And partly because she smelt of freshly-baked bread, and reminded him of his grandmother. And partly because she was lonely and sometimes a boy of twelve can sense loneliness better than an adult. And partly because he was a little different from other children.

By the middle of October, when there was only a fortnight left for the school to close, the first snow had fallen on the distant mountains. One peak stood high above the rest, a white pinnacle against the azure-blue sky. When the sun set, this peak turned from orange to gold to pink to red.

'How high is that mountain?' asked Anil.

'It must be over twelve thousand feet,' replied Miss Mackenzie. 'About thirty miles from here, as the crow flies. I always wanted to go there, but there was no proper road. At that height, there'll be flowers that you don't get here—the blue gentian and the purple columbine, the anemone and the edelweiss.'

'I'll go there one day,' said Anil.

'I'm sure you will, if you really want to.'

The day before his school closed, Anil came to say goodbye to Miss Mackenzie.

'I don't suppose you'll be able to find many wild flowers in Delhi,' she said. 'But have a good holiday.'

'Thank you, miss.'

As he was about to leave, Miss Mackenzie, on an impulse, thrust the *Flora Himaliensis* into his hands.

'You keep it,' she said. 'It's a present for you.'

'But I'll be back next year, and I'll be able to look at it then. It's so valuable.'

'I know it's valuable and that's why I've given it to you. Otherwise it will only fall into the hands of the junk dealers.'

'But, miss . . .'

'Don't argue. Besides, I may not be here next year.'

'Are you going away?'

'I'm not sure. I may go to England.'

She had no intention of going to England; she had not seen the country since she was a child, and she knew she would not fit in with the life of post-war Britain. Her home was in these hills, among the oaks and maples and deodars. It was lonely, but at her age it would be lonely anywhere.

The boy tucked the book under his arm, straightened his tie, stood stiffly to attention and said, 'Goodbye, Miss Mackenzie.'

It was the first time he had spoken her name.

Winter set in early and strong winds brought rain and sleet, and soon there were no flowers in the garden or on the hillside. The cat stayed indoors, curled up at the foot of Miss Mackenzie's bed.

Miss Mackenzie wrapped herself up in all her old shawls and mufflers, but still she felt the cold. Her fingers grew so stiff that she took almost an hour to open a can of baked beans. And then it snowed and for several days the milkman did not come. The postman arrived with her pension papers, but she felt too tired to take them up to town to the bank.

She spent most of the time in bed. It was the warmest place. She kept a hot-water bottle at her back, and the cat kept her feet warm. She lay in bed, dreaming of the spring and summer months. In three months the primroses would be out, and with the coming of spring the boy would return.

One night the hot-water bottle burst and the bedding was soaked through. As there was no sun for several days, the blanket remained damp. Miss Mackenzie caught a chill and had to keep to her cold, uncomfortable bed. She knew she had a fever but there was no thermometer with which to take her temperature. She had difficulty in breathing.

A strong wind sprang up one night, and the window flew open and kept banging all night. Miss Mackenzie was too weak to get up and close it, and the wind swept the rain and sleet into the room. The cat crept into the bed and snuggled close to its mistress's warm body. But towards morning that body had lost its warmth and the cat left the bed and started scratching about on the floor.

As a shaft of sunlight streamed through the open window, the milkman arrived. He poured some milk into the cat's saucer on the doorstep, and the cat leapt down from the windowsill and made for the milk.

The milkman called a greeting to Miss Mackenzie, but received no answer. Her window was open and he had always known her to be up before sunrise. So he put his head in at the window and called again. But Miss Mackenzie did not answer. She had gone away to the mountain where the blue gentian and purple columbine grew.

A Tiger in the House

Timothy, the tiger cub, was discovered by Grandfather on a hunting expedition in the Terai jungle near Dehra.

Grandfather was no shikari, but as he knew the forests of the Siwalik Hills better than most people, he was persuaded to accompany the party—it consisted of several Very Important Persons from Delhi—to advise on the terrain and the direction the beaters should take once a tiger had been spotted.

The camp itself was sumptuous—seven large tents (one for each shikari), a dining tent, and a number of tents for servants. The dinner was very good, as Grandfather admitted afterwards; it was not often that one saw hot-water plates, finger glasses, and seven or eight courses in a tent in the jungle! But that was how things were done in the days of viceroys . . . There were also some fifteen elephants, four of them with howdahs for the shikaris, and the others specially trained for taking part in the beat.

The sportsmen never saw a tiger, nor did they shoot anything else, though they saw a number of deer, peacock and wild boar. They were giving up all hope of finding a tiger, and were beginning to shoot at jackals, when Grandfather, strolling down the forest path at some distance from the rest of the party, discovered a little tiger cub, about eighteen inches long, hiding among the intricate roots of a banyan tree. Grandfather picked him up and brought him home after the camp had broken up. He had the distinction of being the only member of the party to have bagged any game, dead or alive.

At first the tiger cub, who was named Timothy by Grandmother, was brought up entirely on milk given to him in a feeding bottle by our cook Mahmoud. But the milk proved too rich for him, and he was put on a diet of raw mutton and cod liver oil, to be followed later by a more tempting diet of pigeons and rabbits.

Timothy was provided with two companions—Toto the monkey, who was bold enough to pull the young tiger by the tail, and then climb up the curtains if Timothy lost his temper; and a small mongrel puppy, found on the road by Grandfather one day.

At first Timothy appeared to be quite afraid of the puppy, and darted back with a spring if it came too near. He would make absurd dashes at it with his large forepaws, and then retreat to a ridiculously safe distance. Finally, he allowed the puppy to crawl on his back and rest there!

One of Timothy's favourite amusements was to stalk anyone who would play with him and so, when I came to live with Grandfather, I became one of the tiger's favourites. With a crafty look in his glittering eyes, and his body crouching, Timothy would creep closer and closer to me, suddenly making a dash for my feet, rolling over on his back, kicking with delight, and pretending to bite my ankles.

He was by this time the size of a full-grown retriever, and

when I took him out for walks, people on the road would give us a wide berth. When he pulled hard on his chain, I had difficulty in keeping up with him. His favourite place in the house was the drawing room, and he would make himself comfortable on the long sofa, reclining there with great dignity, and snarling at anybody who tried to get him off.

Timothy had clean habits, and would scrub his face with his paws exactly like a cat. He slept at night in the cook's quarters, and was always delighted at being let out by him in the morning.

'One of these days,' declared Grandmother in her prophetic manner, 'we are going to find Timothy sitting on Mahmoud's bed and no sign of the cook except his clothes and shoes!'

Of course, it never came to that, but when Timothy was about six months old a change came over him; he grew steadily less friendly. When out for a walk with me, he would try to steal away to stalk a cat or someone's pet Pekinese; sometimes at night we would hear frenzied cackling from the poultry house, and in the morning there would be feathers lying all over the veranda. Timothy had to be chained up more often. And, finally, when he began to stalk Mahmoud about the house with what looked like villainous intent, Grandfather decided it was time to transfer him to a zoo.

The nearest zoo was at Lucknow, two hundred miles away. Reserving a first-class compartment for himself and Timothy— no one would share a compartment with them—Grandfather took him to Lucknow where the zoo authorities were only too glad to receive as a gift a well fed and fairly civilized tiger.

About six months later, when my grandparents were visiting relatives in Lucknow, Grandfather took the opportunity of calling at the zoo to see how Timothy was getting on. I was not there to accompany him, but I heard all about it when he returned to Dehra.

Arriving at the zoo, Grandfather made straight for the particular cage in which Timothy had been interned. The tiger was there, crouched in a corner, full-grown and with a magnificent striped coat.

'Hello Timothy,' called Grandfather and, climbing the railing with ease, he put his arm through the bars of the cage.

The tiger approached the bars, and allowed Grandfather to put both hands around his head. Grandfather stroked the tiger's forehead and tickled his ear, and, whenever he growled, smacked him across the mouth, which was his old way of keeping Timothy quiet.

He licked Grandfather's hands and only sprang away when a leopard in the next cage snarled at him. Grandfather shooed the leopard away, and the tiger returned to lick his hands; but every now and then the leopard would rush at the bars, and the tiger would slink back to his corner.

A number of people had gathered to watch the reunion when a keeper pushed his way through the crowd and asked Grandfather what he was doing.

'I'm talking to Timothy,' answered Grandfather calmly. 'Weren't you here when I gave him to the zoo six months ago?'

'I haven't been here very long,' replied the surprised keeper.

'Please continue your conversation. But I have never been able to touch him myself, he is always very bad-tempered.'

'Why don't you put him somewhere else?' suggested Grandfather. 'That leopard keeps frightening him. I'll go and see the Superintendent about it.'

Grandfather went in search of the Superintendent of the zoo, but found that he had gone home early; and so, after wandering about the zoo for a little while, he returned to Timothy's cage to say goodbye. It was beginning to get dark.

He had been stroking and slapping Timothy for about five minutes when he found another keeper observing him with some alarm. Grandfather recognized him as the keeper who had been there when Timothy had first come to the zoo.

'*You* remember me,' said Grandfather. 'Now why don't you transfer Timothy to another cage, away from this stupid leopard?'

'But ... Sir ... ' stammered the keeper, 'this is not your tiger.'

'I know, I know,' said Grandfather testily. 'I realize he is no longer mine. But you might at least take a suggestion or two from me.'

'I remember your tiger very well,' said the keeper. 'He died two months ago.'

'Died!' exclaimed Grandfather.

'Yes, sir, of pneumonia. This tiger was trapped in the hills only last month, and he is very dangerous!'

Grandfather could think of nothing to say. The tiger was still licking his arm, with increasing relish. Grandfather took what seemed to him an age to withdraw his hand from the cage.

With his face near the tiger's he mumbled, 'Goodnight, Timothy,' and giving the keeper a scornful look, walked briskly out of the zoo.

The Window

I came in the spring, and took the room on the roof. It was a long, low building which housed several families; the roof was flat, except for my room and a chimney. I don't know whose room owned the chimney, but my room owned the roof. And from the window of my room I owned the world.

But only from the window.

The banyan tree, just opposite, was mine, and its inhabitants my subjects. They were two squirrels, a few mynah, a crow and at night, a pair of flying foxes. The squirrels were busy in the afternoons, the birds in the mornings and evenings, the foxes at night. I wasn't very busy that year, not as busy as the inhabitants of the banyan tree.

There was also a mango tree but that came later, in the summer, when I met Koki and the mangoes were ripe.

At first, I was lonely in my room. But then I discovered the power of my window. I looked out on the banyan tree, on the garden, on the broad path that ran beside the building, and out over the roofs of other houses, over roads and fields, as far as the horizon. The path was not a very busy one but it held variety: an ayah, with a baby in a pram; the postman, an event in himself; the fruit seller, the toy seller, calling their wares in high-pitched familiar cries; the rent collector; a posse of cyclists; a long chain of schoolgirls; a lame beggar . . . all passed my way, the way of my window . . .

In the early summer, a tonga came rattling and jingling down the path and stopped in front of the house. A girl and an elderly lady climbed down, and a servant unloaded their baggage. They went into the house and the tonga moved off, the horse snorting a little.

The next morning the girl looked up from the garden and saw me at my window.

She had long, black hair that fell to her waist, tied with a single red ribbon. Her eyes were black like her hair and just as shiny. She must have been about ten or eleven years old.

'Hello,' I called with a friendly smile.

She looked suspiciously at me. 'Who are you?' she said.

'I'm a ghost.'

She laughed, and her laugh had a gay, mocking quality. 'You look like one!'

I didn't think her remark particularly flattering, but I had asked for it. I stopped smiling anyway. Most children don't like adults smiling at them all the time.

'What have you got up there?' she asked.

'Magic,' I said.

She laughed again but this time without mockery. 'I don't believe you,' she said.

'Why don't you come up and see for yourself?'

She hesitated a little but came round to the steps and began climbing them, slowly, cautiously. And when she entered the room, she brought a magic of her own.

'Where's your magic?' she asked, looking me in the eye.

'Come here,' I said, and I took her to the window and showed her the world.

She said nothing but stared out of the window uncomprehendingly at first, and then with increasing interest. And after some time she turned around and smiled at me, and we were friends.

I only knew that her name was Koki, and that she had come with her aunt to the hills for the summer months; I didn't need to know any more about her, and she didn't need to know anything about me except that I wasn't really a ghost—not the frightening sort anyway . . .

She came up my steps nearly every day and joined me at the window. There was a lot of excitement to be had in our world, especially when the rains broke.

At the first rumblings, women would rush outside to retrieve the washing from the clothes line and if there was a breeze, to chase a few garments across the compound. When the rains came, they came with a vengeance, making a bog of the garden and a river of the path. A cyclist would come riding furiously down the path, an elderly gentleman would be having difficulty with an umbrella and naked children would be frisking about in the rain. Sometimes Koki would run out to the roof, and shout and dance in the rain.

And the rain would come through the open door and window of the room, flooding the floor and making an island of the bed.

But the window was more fun than anything else. It gave us the power of detachment: we were deeply interested in the life around us, but not involved in it.

'It is like a cinema,' said Koki. 'The window is the screen, the world is the picture.'

Soon the mangoes were ripe, and Koki was in the branches of the mango tree as often as she was in my room. From the window I had a good view of the tree, and we spoke to each other from the same height. We ate far too many mangoes, at least five a day.

'Let's make a garden on the roof,' suggested Koki. She was full of ideas like this.

'And how do you propose to do that?' I asked.

'It's easy. We bring up mud and bricks and make the flower beds. Then we plant the seeds. We'll grow all sorts of flowers.'

'The roof will fall in,' I predicted.

But it didn't. We spent two days carrying buckets of mud up the steps to the roof and laying out the flower beds. It was very hard work, but Koki did most of it. When the beds were ready, we had the opening ceremony. Apart from a few small plants collected from the garden below, we had only one species of seeds—pumpkin.

We planted the pumpkin seeds in the mud, and felt proud of ourselves.

But it rained heavily that night, and in the morning I discovered that everything—except the bricks—had been washed away.

So we returned to the window.

A mynah had been in a fight—with a crow perhaps—and the feathers had been knocked off its head. A bougainvillea that had been climbing the wall had sent a long, green shoot in through the window.

Koki said, 'Now we can't shut the window without spoiling the creeper.'

'Then we will never close the window,' I answered.

And so we let the creeper into the room.

The rains passed, and an autumn wind came whispering through the branches of the banyan tree. There were red leaves on the ground, and the wind picked them up and blew them about, so that they looked like butterflies. I would watch the sun rise in the morning, the sky all red until its first rays splashed the windowsill and crept up the walls of the room. And in the evening, Koki and I watched the sun go down in a sea of fluffy clouds; sometimes the clouds were pink and sometimes orange; they were always coloured clouds framed in the window.

'I'm going tomorrow,' announced Koki one evening.

I was too surprised to say anything.

'You stay here forever, don't you?' she said.

I remained silent.

'When I come again next year you will still be here, won't you?'

'I don't know,' I replied. 'But the window will still be here.'

'Oh, do be here next year,' she said, 'or someone will close the window!'

In the morning the tonga was at the door, and the servant, the aunt and Koki were in it. Koki waved to me at my window.

The Window

Then the driver flicked the reins, the wheels of the carriage creaked and rattled, the bell jingled. Down the path went the tonga, down the path and through the gate, and all the time Koki waved; and from the gate I must have looked like a ghost, standing alone at the high window, amongst the bougainvillea.

When the tonga was out of sight, I took the spray of bougainvillea in my hand and pushed it out of the room. Then I closed the window. It would be opened only when the spring and Koki returned.

A Song for Lost Friends

1

As a boy I stood on the edge of the railway cutting,
Outside the dark tunnel, my hands touching
The hot rails, waiting for them to tremble
At the coming of the noonday train.
The whistle of the engine hung on the forest's silence.
Then out of the tunnel, a green-gold dragon
Came plunging, thundering past—
Out of the tunnel, out of the grinning dark.

And the train rolled on, every day
Hundreds of people coming or going or running away—
Goodbye, goodbye!
I haven't seen you again, bright boy at the carriage window,
Waving to me, calling,
But I've loved you all these years and looked for you
everywhere,

In cities and villages, beside the sea,
In the mountains, in crowds at distant places;
Returning always to the forest's silence,
To watch the windows of some passing train . . .

2

My father took me by the hand and led me
Among the ruins of old forts and palaces.
We lived in a tent near the tomb of Humayun,
Among old trees. Now multi-storeyed blocks
Rise from the plain—tomorrow's ruins . . .
You can explore them, my son, when the trees
Take over again and the thorn apple grows
In empty windows. There were seven cities before . . .

Nothing my father said could bring my mother home;
She had gone with another. He took me to the hills
In a small train, the engine having palpitations
As it toiled up the steep slopes peopled
With pines and rhododendrons. Through tunnels
To Shimla. Boarding school. He came to see me
In the holidays. We caught butterflies together.
'Next year,' he said, 'when the War is over,
We'll go to England.' But wars are never over
And I have yet to go to England with my father.

He died that year
And I was dispatched to my mother and stepfather—
A long journey through a dark tunnel.

No one met me at the station. So I wandered
Round Dehra in a tonga, looking for a house
With litchi trees. She'd written to say there were litchi
in the garden.
But in Dehra all the houses had litchi trees,
The tonga driver charged five rupees
For taking me back to the station.
They were looking for me on the platform:
'We thought the train would be late as usual.'
It had arrived on time, upsetting everyone's schedule.

In my new home I found a new baby in a new pram.
Your little brother, they said; which made me a hundred.
But he too was left behind with the servants
When my mother and Mr H. went hunting
Or danced late at the casino, our only wartime nightclub.
Tommies and Yanks scuffled drunk and disorderly
In a private war for the favours of stale women.

Lonely in the house with the servants and the child
And books I'd read twice and my father's letters

134

Treasured secretly in the small trunk beneath my bed:
I wrote to him once but did not post the letter
For fear it might come back 'Return to sender . . .'

One day I slipped into the guava orchard next door—
It really belonged to Seth Hari Kishore
Who'd gone to the Ganga on a pilgrimage—
The guavas were ripe and ready for boys to steal
(Always sweeter when stolen)
And a bare leg thrust at me as I climbed:

'There's only room for one,' came a voice.
I looked up at a boy who had blackberry eyes
And guava juice on his chin, grabbed at him
And we both tumbled out of the tree
On to the ragged December grass. We rolled and fought
But not for long. A gardener came shouting,
And we broke and ran—over the gate and down the road
And across the fields and a dry riverbed,
Into the shades of afternoon . . .
'Why didn't you run home?' he said.
'Why didn't you?'
'There's no one there, my mother's out.'
'And mine's at home.'

3

His mother was Burmese; his father
An English soldier killed in the War.
They were waiting for it to be over.
Every day, beyond the gardens, we loafed:
Time was suspended for a time.
On heavy wings, ringed pheasants rose
At our approach.
The fields were yellow with mustard,
Parrots wheeled in the sunshine, dipped and disappeared
Into the morning mist on the foothills.
We found a pool, fed by a freshet
Of cold spring water. 'One day when we are men,'
He said, 'we'll meet here at the pool again.
'Promise?' 'Promise,' I said. And we took a pledge.
In blood, nicking our fingers on a penknife
And pressing them to each other's lips. Sweet salty kiss.
Late evening, past cowdust time, we trudged home:
He to his mother, I to my dinner.

One wining-dancing night I thought I'd stay out too.
We went to the pictures—*Gone with the Wind*—
A crashing bore for boys, and it finished late.
So I had dinner with them, and his mother said:
'It's past ten. You'd better stay the night.
But will they miss you?'

I did not answer but climbed into my friend's bed—
I'd never slept with anyone before, except my father—
And when it grew cold, after midnight,
He put his arms around me and looped a leg
Over mine and it was nice that way.
But I stayed awake with the niceness of it
My sleep stolen by his own deep slumber . . .
What dreams were lost, I'll never know!
But next morning, just as we'd started breakfast,
A car drew up, and my parents, outraged,
Chastised me for staying out and hustled me home.
Breakfast unfinished. My friend unhappy. My pride wounded.
We met sometimes, but a constraint had grown upon us,
And the following month I heard he'd gone
To an orphanage in Kalimpong.

4

I remember you well, old banyan tree,
As you stood there spreading quietly
Over the broken wall.
While adults slept, I crept away
Down the broad veranda steps, around
The outhouse and the melon ground . . .
In that winter of long ago, I roamed
The faded garden of my mother's home.

I must have known that giants have few friends
(The great lurk shyly in their private dens),
And found you hidden by a thick, green wall
Of aerial roots.
Intruder in your pillared den, I stood
And shyly touched your old and wizened wood,
And as my heart explored you, giant tree,
I heard you singing!

The spirit of the tree became my friend,
Took me to his silent throbbing heart
And taught me the value of stillness.
My first tutor; friend of the lonely.

And the second was the tonga-man
Whose pony cart came rattling along the road
Under the furthest arch of the banyan tree.
Looking up, he waved his whip at me
And laughing, called, 'Who lives up there?'
'I do,' I said.
And the next time he came along, he stopped the tonga
And asked me if I felt lonely in the tree.
'Only sometimes,' I said. 'When the tree is thinking.'
'I never think,' he said. 'You won't feel lonely with me.'
And with a flick of the reins he rattled away,

With a promise he'd give me a ride someday.
And from him I learnt the value of promises kept.

5

From the tree to the tonga was an easy drop.
I fell into life. Bansi, tonga driver,
Wore a yellow waistcoat and spat red
Betel juice the entire width of the road.
'I can spit further than any man,' he claimed.
It is natural for a man to strive to excel
At something; he spat with authority.

When he took me for rides, he lost a fare.
That was his way. He once said, 'If a girl
Wants five rupees for a fix, bargain like hell
And then give six.'
It was the secret of his failure, he claimed,
To give away more than he owned.
And to prove it, he borrowed my pocket money
In order to buy a present for his mistress.

A man who fails well is better than one who succeeds badly.

The rattletrap tonga and the winding road
Through the valley, to the river bed,

With the wind in my hair and the dust
Rising, and the dogs running and barking

And Bansi singing and shouting in my ear,
And the pony farting as it cantered along,
Wheels creaking, seat shifting,

Hood slipping off, the entire contraption
Always about to disintegrate, collapse,
But never quite doing so—like the man himself . . .
All this was music,
And the ragtime-raga lingers in my mind.

Nostalgia comes swiftly when one is forty,
Looking back at boyhood years.
Even unhappiness acquires a certain glow.

It was shady in the cemetery, and the mango trees
Did well there, nourished by the bones
Of long-dead Colonels, Collectors, Magistrates and
Memsahibs.
For here, in dusty splendour, lay the graves
Of those who'd brought their English dust
To lie with Ganges soil: some tombs were temples,
Some were cenotaphs; and one, a tiny Taj.
Here lay sundry relatives, including Uncle Henry,

Who'd been for many years a missionary.
'Sacred to the Memory
Of Henry C. Wagstaff',
Who translated the Gospels into Pashtu,
And was murdered by his own chowkidar.

'Well done, thou good and faithful servant'—
So ran his epitaph.

The gardener, who looked after the trees,
Also dug graves. One day
I found him working at the bottom of a new cavity,
'They never let me know in time,' he grumbled.
'Last week I dug two graves, and now, without warning,
Here's another. It isn't even the season for dying.
There's enough work all summer, when cholera's about—
Why can't they keep alive through the winter?'
Near the railway lines, watching the trains
(There were six every day, coming or going),
And across the line, the leper colony . . .
I did not know they were lepers till later
But I knew they were different: some
Were without fingers or toes
And one had no nose
And a few had holes in their faces
And yet some were beautiful

They had their children with them
And the children were no different
From other children.
I made friends with some
And won most of their marbles
And carried them home in my pockets.

One day my parents found me
Playing near the leper colony.
There was a big scene.
My mother shouted at the lepers
And they hung their heads as though it was all their fault,
And the children had nothing to say.
I was taken home in disgrace
And told all about leprosy and given a bath.
My clothes were thrown away
And the servants wouldn't touch me for days.
So I took the marbles I'd won
And put them in my stepfather's cupboard,
Hoping he'd catch leprosy from them.

6

A slim, dark youth with quiet
Eyes and a gentle, quizzical smile,
Manohar. Fifteen, working in a small hotel.

142

He'd come from the hills and wanted to return,
I forget how we met
But I remember walking the dusty roads
With this gentle boy, who held my hand
And told me about his home, his mother,
His village, and the little river
At the bottom of the hill where the water

Ran blue and white and wonderful,
'When I go home, I'll take you with me.'
But we hadn't enough money.
So I sold my bicycle for thirty rupees
And left a note in the dining room:
'Going away. Don't worry—(hoping they would)—
I'll come home
When I've grown up.'

We crossed the rushing waters of the Ganga
Where they issued from the doors of Vishnu
Then took the pilgrim road, in those days
Just a stony footpath into the mountains:
Not all who ventured forth returned;
Some came to die, of course,
Near the sacred waters or at their source.
We took this route and spent a night
At a wayside inn, wrapped tight

143

In the single blanket I'd brought along;
Even then we were cold
It was not the season for pilgrims
And the inn was empty, except for the locals
Drinking a local brew.

We drank a little and listened
To an old soldier from the hills
Talking of the women he'd known
In the first Great War, when stationed in Rome;
His memories were good for many drinks
In many inns; his face pickled in the suns
Of many mountain summers.
The mule drivers slept in one room
And talked all night over hookahs.
Manohar slept bravely, but I lay watching
A bright star through the tiny window
And wished upon it, already knowing that wishes
Had no power, but wishing all the same . . .
And next morning we set off again
Leaving the pilgrim-route to march
Down a valley, above a smaller river,
Walking until I felt
We'd walk and walk for ever.
Late at night, on a cold mountain,

Two lonely figures, we saw the lights
Of scattered houses and knew we had arrived.

7

'Not death, but a summing-up of life,'
Said the village patriarch, as we watched him
Treasure a patch of winter sunshine
On his string cot in the courtyard.
I remember his wisdom.
And I remember faces.
For its faces I remember best.
The people were poor, and the patriarch said:
'I have heard it told that the sun
Sets in splendour in Himalaya—
But who can eat sunsets?'

Perhaps, if I'd stayed longer,
I would have yearned for creature comforts.
We were hungry sometimes, eating wild berries
Or slyly milking another's goat,
Or catching small fish in the river . . .
But I did not long for home.
Could I have grown up a village boy,
Grazing sheep and cattle, while the *Collected Works*
Of W. Shakespeare lay gathering dust

In Dehra? Who knows? But it was nice
Of my stepfather to send his office manager
Into the mountains to bring me home!

Manohar.
He called goodbye and waved
As I looked back from the bend in the road.
Bright boy on the mountainside,
Waving to me, calling, and I've loved you
All these years and looked for you everywhere,
In the mountains, in crowds at distant places,
In cities and villages, beside the sea.
And the trains roll on, every day
Hundreds of people coming or going or running away—
Goodbye, goodbye!
Into the forest's silence,
Outside the dark tunnel,
Out of the tunnel, out of the dark . . .

When the Guavas Are Ripe

Guava trees are easy to climb. And guavas are good to eat. So it's little wonder that an orchard of guava trees is a popular place with boys and girls.

Just across the road from Ranji's house, on the other side of a low wall, was a large guava orchard. The monsoon rains were almost over. It was a warm, humid day in September, and the guavas were ripening, turning from green to gold; no longer hard, but growing soft and sweet and juicy.

The schools were closed for a few days because of a religious festival. Ranji's father was at work in his office. Ranji's mother was enjoying an afternoon siesta on a stretcher in the backyard. His grandmother was busy teaching her pet parrot to recite a prayer.

'I feel like getting on to those guava trees,' said Ranji to himself. 'It's been months since I climbed a tree!'

He was soon across the road and over the wall and into the orchard. He chose a tree that grew in the middle of the orchard, where it was unlikely he would be disturbed. He climbed swiftly into its branches. A cluster of guavas swung just above him. He reached up for one of them, but to his surprise found himself clutching a small bare foot which had suddenly been thrust through the foliage.

Having caught the foot, Ranji did not let go. Instead, he pulled hard on it. There was a squeal and someone came toppling down on him. Ranji found himself clutching at arms and legs. Together the two bodies crashed through a couple of branches and landed with a thud on the soft ground beneath the tree.

Ranji and the interloper struggled fiercely. They rolled about on the grass. Ranji tried to do a judo hold—without any success. Then he saw that his opponent was a girl. It was his friend and neighbour, Koki.

'It's you!' he gasped.

'It's me,' said Koki. 'And what are *you* doing here?'

'Get your knee out of my stomach and I'll tell you.' When Ranji had recovered his breath, he said, 'I just felt like climbing a tree.'

'So did I.'

He just stared at her. There was guava juice at the corners of her mouth and on her chin.

'Are the guavas good?' he asked.

'Quite sweet in this tree,' said Koki. 'You find another tree for yourself, Ranji. There must be thirty or forty trees to choose from.'

'And all going to waste,' said Ranji. 'Look, some of the guavas have been spoilt by the birds.'

'Nobody else wants them, it seems.'

Koki climbed back into her tree, and Ranji obligingly walked a little further and climbed another tree. They could still talk to each other without having to shout. But after a few polite exchanges they fell silent, their attention given over entirely to the eating of guavas.

'I've eaten five,' announced Koki after some time.

'You'd better stop.'

'You're only saying that because you've just started.'

'Well, three's enough for me.'

'I'm getting a tummy ache, I think.'

'I warned you. Come on, I'll take you home. We can come back tomorrow. There are still lots of guavas left. Hundreds!'

'I don't think I want to eat any more,' said Koki.

She felt better the next day—so well, in fact, that Ranji found her leaning on the gate, waiting for him to join her. She was accompanied by her smaller brother, Teju, who was only six and very mischievous.

'How are you feeling today?' Ranji asked.

'Hungry,' said Koki.

'Why did you bring your brother?'

'He wants to climb trees.'

Soon they were in the orchard. Ranji and Koki helped Teju into the branches of one of the smaller trees and then made for other trees, disturbing a party of parrots, who flew in circles around the orchard, screaming their protests.

Two boys and a girl talking to each other from three different trees can make quite a lot of noise, and it wasn't only the birds who were disturbed.

Though they did not know it, the orchard belonged to a wealthy property dealer, and he employed a gardener-cum-watchman, whose duty was to keep away birds, children, monkeys, flying foxes and other fruit-eating pests. But on a hot, sultry afternoon, Gopal the watchman could not resist taking a nap. He was stretched out under a shady jackfruit tree, snoring so loudly that the flies who had been buzzing round him felt that a storm was brewing and kept their distance.

Gopal woke to the sound of voices raised high in glee. Sitting up, he brushed a ladybird from his long moustache, and then seized his *lathi*, a long, stout stick usually carried by watchmen.

'Who's there?' he shouted, struggling to his feet.

There was a sudden silence in the trees.

'Who's there?' Gopal called again.

No answer.

'I must have been dreaming,' he muttered. He was preparing to lie down and take another nap when Teju, who had been watching him, burst into laughter.

'Ho!' shouted the watchman, coming to life again. 'Thieves! I'll settle you!' And he began striding towards the centre of the orchard, boasting all the time of his physical prowess. 'I'm not afraid of thieves, bandits or wild beasts! I'll have you know that I was once the wrestling champion of the entire district of Dehra. Come on out and fight me if you dare!'

'Run!' hissed Koki, scrambling down from her tree.

'Run!' shouted Ranji, as though it was a cricket match.

Teju was so startled by the sudden activity that he tumbled out of his tree and began crying. Ranji and Koki had to go to his aid.

The sight of an enormous ex-wrestler bearing down on them was enough to make Teju stop crying and scramble to his feet. Then all three were fleeing across the orchard, the watchman a little way behind them, waving his lathi and shouting at the top of his voice. But although he was an ex-wrestler (or perhaps because of it), he could not run very fast, and was still huffing and puffing some twenty metres behind when they climbed over the wall. Gopal could not climb walls either.

The children ran off in different directions before returning home.

The next day, Ranji met Koki and Teju at the far end of the road.

'Is he there?' asked Koki.

'I haven't seen him. But he must be around somewhere.'

'Maybe he's gone for his lunch. We'll just walk past and take a quick look.'

The three of them strolled casually down the road. Koki said the gardens were looking very pretty. Teju gazed admiringly at a boy flying a kite from a rooftop. Ranji kept one eye on the road and one eye on the orchard wall. A squirrel ran along the top of the wall; the parrots were back in the guava trees.

They moved closer to the wall. Ranji leaned casually against it and Koki began picking little daisies growing at the edge of the road. Teju, unable to hide his curiosity, pulled himself up on the wall and looked over. At the same time, Gopal the watchman, who had been hiding behind the wall, waiting for them, stood up slowly and gazed fiercely at Teju.

Teju gulped, but did not flinch. He looked straight into the watchman's angry red eyes.

'And what can I do for you?' growled Gopal.

'I was just looking,' said Teju.

'At what?'

'At the view.'

Gopal was a little baffled. They looked just like the children he'd chased away yesterday, but he couldn't be sure. They didn't *look* guilty. But did children ever look guilty?

'There's a better view from the other side of the road,' he said gruffly. 'Now be off!'

'What lovely guavas,' put in Koki, smiling sweetly. There weren't many people who could resist that smile.

'True,' added Ranji, with the air of one who was an expert on guavas and all things horticultural. 'They are just the right size and colour. I don't think I've seen better. But they'll all be spoilt by the birds if you don't gather them soon.'

'It's none of your business,' said the watchman.

'Just look at his muscles,' said Teju, trying a different approach. 'He's really strong!'

Gopal looked pleased for once. He was proud of his former prowess, even though he was now rather flabby around the waist.

'You look like a wrestler,' said Ranji.

'I *am* a wrestler,' answered Gopal.

'I told you so,' said Koki, 'what else could he be?'

'I'm a retired wrestler,' said Gopal.

'You don't look retired,' put in Teju, fast learning that flattery can get you almost anywhere.

Gopal swelled with pride—such admiration hadn't come his way for a long time. To Koki he looked like a bullfrog swelling up, but she thought it was better not to say so.

'Do you want to see my muscles?' he asked.

'Yes, yes!' they cried. 'Do show us.'

Gopal peeled off his shirt and thumped his chest. It sounded like a drum. They were really impressed. Then he bent his elbow and his biceps stood up like cricket balls.

'You can touch them,' he said generously.

Teju poked his finger into Gopal's biceps.

'Mister Universe!' He exclaimed.

Gopal glowed all over. He liked these children. How intelligent they were! Not everyone had the sense to appreciate his strength, his manliness, his magnificent figure!

'Climb over the wall and join me,' he said. 'Come sit on the grass and I'll tell you about the time when I was a wrestling champion.'

Over the wall they came, and sat politely on the grass. Gopal told them about some of his exploits—how he had vanquished a world-famous wrestler in five seconds flat, and how he had saved a carload of travellers from drowning by single-handedly dragging their car out of the river. The children listened patiently. Then Teju mentioned that he was feeling hungry.

'Hungry?' said Gopal. 'Why didn't you tell me before? I'll bring you some guavas, that's all there is to eat here. I know which tree has the best ones. And they're all going to rot if no one eats them. No one's buying the crop this year—the owner's price is too high!'

Gopal hurried off and soon returned with a basket full of guavas.

'Help yourselves,' he offered. 'But don't eat too many or you'll get sick.'

So they munched guavas and listened as Gopal told them about the time he was waylaid by three bandits and how he threw them all into the village pond.

'Will you come again tomorrow?' asked Gopal eagerly, when the guavas were finished and the children got up to leave. 'Do come tomorrow, and I'll tell you another story.'

'We'll come tomorrow,' said Teju, looking at all the guava trees still laden with fruit.

Somehow it seemed very important to Gopal that they should visit again. It was lonely in the orchard. Koki sensed this, and said, 'We like your stories . . .'

'They are good stories,' said Ranji. Even if they are not entirely true, he thought.

They climbed over the wall and waved goodbye to Gopal.

The children came again the next day.

And even when the guava season was over and Gopal had nothing to offer them but his stories, they went to see him because by that time they had grown to like him.

From Small Beginnings

And the last puff of the day-wind brought from the unseen villages the scent of damp woodsmoke, hot cakes, dripping undergrowth, and rotting pine-cones. That is the true smell of the Himalayas, and if once it creeps into the blood of a man, that man will at the last, forgetting all else, return to the hills to die.

—Rudyard Kipling

On the first clear September day, towards the end of the rains, I visited the pine knoll, my place of peace and power.

It was months since I'd last been there. Trips to the plains, a crisis in my affairs, involvements with other people and their troubles, and an entire monsoon had come between me and the grassy, pine-topped slope facing the Hill of Fairies (Pari Tibba to the locals). Now I tramped through late monsoon foliage—tall ferns, bushes festooned with flowering convolvulus—and crossed the stream by way of its little bridge of stones before climbing the steep hill to the pine slope.

When the trees saw me, they made as if to turn in my direction. A puff of wind came across the valley from the distant snows. A long-tailed blue magpie took alarm and flew noisily out of an oak tree. The cicadas were suddenly silent. But the trees remembered me. They bowed gently in the breeze and beckoned me nearer, welcoming me home. Three pines, a straggling oak and a wild cherry. I went among them and acknowledged their welcome with a touch of my hand against their trunks—the cherry's smooth and polished; the pine's patterned and whorled; the oak's rough, gnarled and full of experience. He'd been there longest, and the wind had bent his upper branches and twisted a few, so that he looked shaggy and undistinguished. But like the philosopher who is careless about his dress and appearance, the oak has secrets, a hidden wisdom. He has learnt the art of survival!

While the oak and the pines are older than me and have been here many years, the cherry tree is exactly seven years old. I know, because I planted it.

One day I had this cherry seed in my hand, and on an impulse I thrust it into the soft earth, and then went away and forgot all about it. A few months later I found a tiny cherry tree in the long grass. I did not expect it to survive. But the following year it was two feet tall. And then some goats ate its leaves and a grasscutter's scythe injured the stem, and I was sure it would wither away. But it renewed itself, sprang up even faster, and within three years it was a healthy, growing tree, about five feet tall.

I left the hills for two years—forced by circumstances to make a living in Delhi—but this time I did not forget the cherry tree. I thought about it fairly often, sent telepathic messages of encouragement in its direction. And when, a couple of years ago, I returned in the autumn, my heart did a somersault when I found my tree sprinkled with pale, pink blossoms. (The Himalayan Cherry flowers in November.) And later, when the fruit was ripe, the tree was visited by finches, tits, bulbuls and other small birds, all come to feast on the sour, red cherries.

Last summer I spent a night on the pine knoll, sleeping on the grass beneath the cherry tree. I lay awake for hours, listening to the chatter of the stream and the occasional tonk-tonk of nightjars, and watching through the branches overhead, the stars turning in the sky. And I felt the power of the sky and the earth, and the power of a small cherry seed . . .

And so when the rains are over, this is where I come, that I might feel the peace and power of this place.

This is where I will write my stories. I can see everything from here—my cottage across the valley; behind and above me, the town and the bazaar, straddling the ridge; to the left, the high mountains and the twisting road to the source of the great river; below me, the little stream and the path to the village; ahead, the Pari Tibba and the fields beyond; the wide valley below, and another range of hills and then the distant plains. I can even see Prem Singh in the garden, putting the mattresses out in the sun.

From here he is just a speck on the far hill, but I know it is Prem by the way he stands. A man may have a hundred disguises, but in the end it is his posture that gives him away. Like my grandfather, who was a master of disguise and successfully roamed the bazaars as fruit vendor or basketmaker. But we could always recognize him because of his pronounced slouch.

Prem Singh doesn't slouch, but he has this habit of looking up at the sky (regardless of whether it's cloudy or clear), and at this moment he's looking at the sky.

Eight years with Prem. He was just a sixteen-year-old boy when I first saw him, and now he has a wife and child.

I had been in the cottage for just over a year . . . He stood on the landing outside the kitchen door. A tall boy, dark, with good teeth and brown, deep-set eyes, dressed smartly in white drill—his only change of clothes. Looking for a job. I liked the look of him, but—

'I already have someone working for me,' I said.

'Yes, sir. He is my uncle.'

In the hills, everyone is a brother or an uncle. 'You don't want me to dismiss your uncle?'

'No, sir. But he says you can find a job for me.'

'I'll try. I'll make inquiries. Have you just come from your village?'

'Yes. Yesterday I walked ten miles to Pauri. There I got a bus.'

'Sit down. Your uncle will make some tea.'

He sat down on the steps, removed his white keds, wriggled his toes. His feet were long and broad, large feet but not ugly. He was unusually clean for a hill boy. And taller than most.

'Do you smoke?' I asked.

'No, sir.'

'It is true,' said his uncle. 'He does not smoke. All my nephews smoke but this one. He is a little peculiar, he does not smoke—neither beedi nor hookah.'

'Do you drink?'

'It makes me vomit.'

'Do you take bhang?'

'No, sahib.'

'You have no vices. It's unnatural.'

'He is unnatural, sahib,' said his uncle.

'Does he chase girls?'

'They chase him, sahib.'

'So he left the village and came looking for a job.' I looked at him. The boy grinned, then looked away and began rubbing his feet.

'Your name is . . .?'

'Prem Singh.'

'All right, Prem, I will try to do something for you.'

I did not see him for a couple of weeks. I forgot about finding him work. But when I met him again, on the road to the bazaar, he told me that he had got a temporary job in the Survey, looking after the surveyor's tents.

'Next week we will be going to Rajasthan,' he said.

'It will be very hot. Have you been in the desert before?'

'No, sir.'

'It is not like the hills. And it is far from home.'

'I know. But I have no choice in the matter. I have to collect some money in order to get married.'

In his region there was a bride price, usually of two thousand rupees.

'Do you have to get married so soon?'

'I have only one brother and he is still very young. My mother is not well. She needs a daughter-in-law to help her in the fields and the house, and with the cows. We are a small family, so the work is greater.'

Every family has its few terraced fields, narrow and stony, usually perched on a hillside above a stream or river. They grow rice, barley, maize, potatoes—just enough to live on. Even if their produce is sufficient for marketing, the absence of roads makes it difficult to get the produce to the market towns. There is no money to be earned in the villages, and money is needed for clothes, soap, medicines, and for recovering the family jewellery from the moneylenders. So the young men leave their villages to find work, and to find work they must go to the plains. The lucky ones get into the army. Others enter domestic service or take jobs in garages, hotels, wayside tea shops, schools . . .

In Mussoorie the main attraction is the large number of schools which employ cooks and bearers. But the schools were full when Prem arrived. He'd been to the recruiting centre at Roorkee, hoping to get into the army; but they found a deformity in his right foot, the result of a bone broken when a landslip had carried him away one dark monsoon night. He was lucky, he said, that it was only his foot and not his head that had been broken.

Prem came to the house to inform his uncle about the job and to say goodbye. I thought, another nice person I probably won't see again; another ship passing in the night, the friendly twinkle of its lights soon vanishing in the darkness. I said 'Come again', held his smile with mine so that I could remember him better, and returned to my study and my typewriter. The typewriter is the repository of a writer's loneliness. It stares unsympathetically back at him every day, doing its best to be discouraging. Maybe I'll go back to the old-fashioned quill pen and marble inkstand; then I can feel like a real writer—Balzac or Dickens—scratching away into the endless reaches of the night . . . Of course, the days and nights are seemingly shorter than they need to be! They must be, otherwise why do we hurry so much and achieve so little, by the standards of the past . . .

Prem goes, disappears into the vast, faceless cities of the

plains, and a year slips by, or rather I do, and then here he is again, thinner and darker and still smiling and still looking for a job. I should have known that hill men don't disappear altogether. The spirit-haunted rocks don't let their people wander too far, lest they lose them forever.

I was able to get him a job in the school. The headmaster's wife needed a cook. I wasn't sure if Prem could cook very well but I sent him along and they said they'd give him a trial. Three days later the headmaster's wife met me on the road and started gushing all over me. She was the type who often gushed.

'We're so grateful to you! Thank you for sending me that lovely boy. He's so polite. And he cooks very well. A little too hot for my husband, but otherwise delicious—just delicious! He's a real treasure—a lovely boy.' And she gave me an arch look—the famous look which she used to captivate all the good-looking young prefects who became prefects, it was said, only if she approved of them.

I wasn't sure that she didn't want something more than a cook, and I only hoped that Prem would give every satisfaction.

He looked cheerful enough when he came to see me on his day off.

'How are you getting on?' I asked.

'Lovely,' he said, using his mistress's favourite expression.

'What do you mean—lovely? Do they like your work?'

'The memsahib likes it. She strokes me on the cheek whenever she enters the kitchen. The sahib says nothing. He takes medicine after every meal.'

'Did he always take medicine—or only now that you're doing the cooking?'

'I am not sure. I think he has always been sick.'

Prem was sleeping in the headmaster's veranda and getting sixty rupees a month. A cook in Delhi got a hundred and sixty. And a cook in Paris or New York got ten times as much. I did not say as much to Prem. He might ask me to get him a job in New York. And that would be the last I saw of him! He, as a cook, might well get a job making curries off-Broadway; I, as a writer, wouldn't get to first base. And only my Uncle Ken knew the secret of how to make a living without actually doing any work. But then, of course, he had four sisters. And each of them was married to a fairly prosperous husband. So Uncle Ken divided his year among them. Three months with Aunt Ruby in Nainital. Three months with Aunt Susie in Kashmir. Three months with my mother (not quite so affluent) in Jamnagar. And three months in the Vet Hospital in Bareilly, where Aunt Mabel ran the hospital for her veterinary husband. In this way he never overstayed his welcome. A sister can look after a brother for just three months at a time and no more. Uncle K had it worked out to perfection.

But I had no sisters and I couldn't live forever on the royalties of a single novel. So I had to write others. So I came to the hills.

The hill men go to the plains to make a living. I had to come to the hills to try and make mine.

'Prem,' I said, 'why don't you work for me?'

'And what about my uncle?'

'He seems ready to desert me any day. His grandfather is ill, he says, and he wants to go home.'

'His grandfather died last year.'

'That's what I mean—he's getting restless. And I don't mind

if he goes. These days he seems to be suffering from a form of sleeping sickness. I have to get up first and make his tea . . .'

Sitting here under the cherry tree, whose leaves are just beginning to turn yellow, I rest my chin on my knees and gaze across the valley to where Prem moves about in the garden. Looking back over the seven years he has been with me, I recall some of the nicest things about him. They come to me in no particular order—just pieces of cinema—coloured slides slipping across the screen of memory . . .

Prem rocking his infant son to sleep—crooning to him, passing his large hand gently over the child's curly head—Prem following me down to the police station when I was arrested (on a warrant from Bombay, charging me with writing an allegedly obscene short story!), and waiting outside until I reappeared, his smile, when I found him in Delhi, his large, irrepressible laughter, most in evidence when he was seeing an old Laurel and Hardy movie.

Of course, there were times when he could be infuriating, stubborn, deliberately pig-headed, sending me little notes of resignation—but I never found it difficult to overlook these little acts of self-indulgence. He had brought much love and laughter into my life, and what more could a lonely man ask for?

It was his stubborn streak that limited the length of his stay in the headmaster's household. Mr Good was tolerant enough. But Mrs Good was one of those women who, when they are pleased with you, go out of their way to help, pamper and flatter, but when displeased, become vindictive, going out of their way to harm or destroy. Mrs Good sought power—over her husband, her dog, her favourite pupils, her servant . . . She had absolute power over the husband and the dog, partial power over her slightly bewildered pupils, and none at all over Prem, who missed the subtleties of her designs upon his soul. He did not respond to her mothering, or to the way in which she tweaked him on the cheeks, brushed against him in the kitchen and made admiring remarks about his looks and physique. Memsahibs, he knew, were not for him. So he kept a stony face and went diligently about his duties. And she felt slighted, put in her place. Her liking turned to dislike. Instead of admiring remarks, she began making disparaging comments about his looks, his clothes, his manners. She found fault with his cooking. No longer was it 'lovely'. She even accused him of taking away the dog's meat and giving it to a poor family living on the hillside—no more heinous crime could be imagined! Mr Good threatened him with dismissal. So Prem became stubborn. The following day he withheld the dog's food altogether, threw it down the khud where it was seized upon by innumerable strays, and went off to the pictures.

That was the end of his job.

'I'll have to go home now,' he told me. 'I won't get another job in this area. The mem will see to that.'

'Stay a few days,' I suggested.

'I have only enough money with which to get home.'

'Keep it for going home. You can stay with me for a few days, while you look around. Your uncle won't mind sharing his food with you.'

His uncle did mind. He did not like the idea of working for his nephew as well; it seemed to him no part of his duties. And he was apprehensive that Prem might get his job.

So Prem stayed no longer than a week.

Here on the knoll the grass is just beginning to turn October yellow. The first clouds approaching winter cover the sky. The trees are very still. The birds are silent. Only a cricket keeps singing on the oak tree. Perhaps there will be a storm before evening. A storm like the one in which Prem arrived at the cottage with his wife and child—but that's jumping too far ahead . . .

After he had returned to his village, it was several months before I saw him again. His uncle told me he had taken up a job in Delhi. There was an address. It did not seem complete, but I resolved that when I was next in Delhi I would try to see him.

The opportunity came in May, as the hot winds of summer blew across the plains. It was the time of year when people who can afford it, try to get away to the hills. I dislike New Delhi at the best of times, and I hate it in summer. People compete with each other in being bad-tempered and mean. But I had to go down—I don't remember why, but it must have seemed very necessary at the time—and I took the opportunity to try and see Prem.

Nothing went right for me. Of course the address was all wrong, and I wandered about in a remote, dusty, treeless colony called Vasant Vihar for over two hours, asking all the domestic servants I came across if they could put me in touch with Prem Singh of Village Koli, Pauri Garhwal. There were innumerable Prem Singhs, but apparently none who belonged to Village Koli. I returned to my hotel and took two days to recover from heatstroke before returning to Mussoorie, thanking God for the mountains!

And then the uncle gave notice. He'd found a better paid job in Dehradun and was anxious to be off. I didn't try to stop him.

For the next six months I lived in the cottage without any help. I did not find this difficult. I was used to living alone. It wasn't service that I needed but companionship. In the cottage it was very quiet. The ghosts of long dead residents were sympathetic but unobtrusive. The song of the whistling thrush was beautiful, but I knew he was not singing for me. Up the valley came the sound of a flute, but I never saw the flute player. My affinity was with the little red fox who roamed the hillside below the cottage. I met him one night and wrote these lines:

As I walked home last night
I saw a lone fox dancing
In the cold moonlight.
I stood and watched—then
Took the low road, knowing
The night was his by right.
Sometimes, when words ring true,
I'm like a lone fox dancing
In the morning dew.

During the rains, watching the dripping trees and the mist climbing the valley, I wrote a great deal of poetry. Loneliness is of value to poets. But poetry didn't bring me much money, and funds were low. And then, just as I was wondering if I would have to give up my freedom and take a job again, a publisher bought the paperback rights of one of my children's stories, and I was free to live and write as I pleased—for another three months!

That was in November. To celebrate, I took a long walk through the Landour bazaar and up the Tehri road. It was a good day for walking; and it was dark by the time I returned to the outskirts of the town. Someone stood waiting for me on the road above the cottage. I hurried past him.

If I am not for myself,
Who will be for me?
And if I am not for others,

What am I?

And if not now, when?

I startled myself with the memory of these words of Hillel, the ancient Hebrew sage. I walked back to the shadows where the youth stood, and saw that it was Prem.

'Prem!' I said. 'Why are you sitting out here, in the cold? Why did you not go to the house?'

'I went, sir, but there was a lock on the door. I thought you had gone away.'

'And you were going to remain here, on the road?'

'Only for tonight. I would have gone down to Dehra in the morning.'

'Come, let's go home. I have been waiting for you. I looked for you in Delhi, but could not find the place where you were working.'

'I have left them now.'

'And your uncle has left me. So will you work for me now?'

'For as long as you wish.'

'For as long as the gods wish.'

We did not go straight home, but returned to the bazaar and took our meal in the Sindhi Sweet Shop—hot puris and strong, sweet tea.

We walked home together in the bright moonlight. I felt sorry for the little fox dancing alone.

That was twenty years ago, and Prem and his wife and three children are still with me. But we live in a different house now, on another hill.

The Canal

We loved to bathe there, on hot summer afternoons—Sushil and Raju and Pitamber and I—and there were others as well, but we were the regulars, the ones who met at other times too, eating at chaat shops or riding on bicycles into the tea gardens.

The canal has disappeared—or rather, it has gone underground, having been covered over with concrete to widen the road to which it ran parallel for most of its way. Here and there it went through a couple of large properties, and it was at the extremity of one of these—just inside the boundaries of Miss Gamla's house—that the canal went into a loop, where it was joined by another small canal, and this was the best place for bathing or just romping around. The smaller boys wore nothing, but we had just reached the years of puberty and kept our kacchas on. So Miss Gamla really had nothing to complain about.

I'm not sure if this was her real name. I think we called her Miss Gamla because of the large number of gamlas or flowerpots that surrounded her house. They filled the veranda, decorated the windows, and lined the approach road. She had a mali who was always watering the pots. And there was no shortage of water, the canal being nearby.

But Miss Gamla did not like small boys. Or big boys, for that matter. She placed us high on her list of Pests, along with monkeys (who raided her kitchen), sparrows (who shattered her sweet peas), and goats (who ate her geraniums). We did none of these things, being strictly fun-loving creatures; but we did make a lot of noise, spoiling her afternoon siesta. And I think she was offended by the sight of our near-naked bodies cavorting about on the boundaries of her estate. A spinster in her sixties, the proximity of naked flesh, no matter how immature, perhaps disturbed and upset her.

She had a companion—a noisy peke, who followed her around everywhere and set up an ear-splitting barking at anyone who came near. It was the barking, rather than our play, that woke her in the afternoons. And then she would emerge from her back veranda, waving a stick at us, and shouting at us to be off.

We would collect our clothes, and lurk behind a screen of lantana bushes, returning to the canal as soon as lady and dog were back in the house.

The canal came down from the foothills, from a hill called Nalapani where a famous battle had taken place a hundred and fifty years back, between the British and the Gurkhas. But for some quirky reason, possibly because we were not very good at history, we called it the Panipat canal, after a more famous battle once fought north of Delhi.

We had our own mock battles, wrestling on the grassy banks of the canal before plunging into the water—it was no more than waist-high—flailing around with shouts of joy, with no one to hinder our animal spirits . . .

Except Miss Gamla.

Down the path she hobbled—she had a pronounced limp—waving her walnut-wood walking stick at us, while her bulging-eyed peke came yapping at her heels.

'Be off, you chhokra-boys!' she'd shout. 'Off to your filthy homes, or I'll put the police on to you!'

And on one occasion she did report us to the local thana, and a couple of policemen came along, told us to get dressed and warned us off the property. But the Head Constable was Pitamber's brother-in-law's brother-in-law, so the ban did not last for more than a couple of days. We were soon back at our favourite stretch of canal.

When Miss Gamla saw that we were back, as merry and disrespectful as ever, she was furious. She nearly had a fit when Raju—probably the most wicked of the four of us—did a jig in front of her, completely in the nude.

When Miss Gamla advanced upon him, stick raised, he jumped into the canal.

'Why don't you join us?' shouted Sushil, taunting the enraged woman.

'Jump in and cool off,' I called, not to be outdone in villainy.

The little peke ran up and down the banks of the canal, yapping furiously, dying to sink its teeth into our bottoms. Miss Gamla came right down to the edge of the canal, waving her stick, trying to connect with any part of Raju's anatomy that could be reached. The ferrule of the stick caught him on the shoulder and he yelped in pain. Miss Gamla gave a shrill cry of delight. She had scored a hit!

She made another lunge at Raju, and this time I caught the end of the stick and pulled. Instead of letting go of the stick,

Miss Gamla hung on to it. I should have let go then, but on an impulse I gave it a short, sharp pull, and to my horror, both walking stick and Miss Gamla tumbled into the canal.

Miss Gamla went under for a few seconds. Then she came to the surface, spluttering, and screamed. There was a frenzy of barking from the peke. Why had he been left out of the game? Wisely, he forbore from joining us.

We went to the aid of Miss Gamla, with every intention of pulling her out of the canal, but she backed away, screaming, 'Get away from me, get away!' Fortunately, the walking stick had been carried away by the current.

Miss Gamla was now in danger of being carried away too. Floundering about, she had backed away to a point where a secondary canal joined the first, and here the current was swift. All the boys, big and small, avoided that spot. It formed a little whirlpool before rushing on.

'Memsahib, be careful!' called out Pitamber.

'Watch out!' I shouted, 'You won't be able to stand against the current.'

Raju and Sushil lunged forward to help, but with a look of hatred Miss Gamla turned away and tried to walk downstream. A surge in the current swept her off her legs. Her gown billowed up, turning her into a sailboat, and she moved slowly downstream, arms flailing as she tried to regain her balance.

We scrambled out of the canal and ran along the bank, hoping to overtake her, but we were hindered by the peke who kept snapping at our heels, and by the fact that we were without our clothes and approaching the busy Dilaram Bazaar.

Just before the Bazaar, the canal went underground, emerging about two hundred metres further on, at the junction of the Old Survey Road and the East Canal Road. To our horror, we saw Miss Gamla float into the narrow tunnel that carried the canal along its underground journey. If she didn't get stuck somewhere in the channel, she would emerge—hopefully, still alive—at the other end of the passage.

We ran back for our clothes, dressed, then ran through the bazaar, and did not stop running until we reached the exit point on the Canal Road. This must have taken ten to fifteen minutes.

We took up our positions on the culvert where the canal emerged, and waited.

We waited and waited.

No sign of Miss Gamla.

'She must be stuck somewhere,' said Pitamber.

'She'll drown,' said Sushil.

'Not our fault,' argued Raju. 'If we tell anyone, we'll get into trouble. They'll think we pushed her in.'

'We'll wait a little longer,' I suggested.

So we hung about the canal banks, pretending to catch tadpoles, and hoping that Miss Gamla would emerge, preferably alive.

Her walking stick floated past. We did not touch it. It would be evidence against us, warned Pitamber. The dog had gone home after seeing his mistress disappear down the tunnel.

'Like Alice,' I thought. 'Only that was a dream.'

When it grew dark, we went our different ways, resolving not to mention the episode to anyone. We might be accused of murder! By now, we *felt* like murderers.

A week passed, and nothing happened. No bloated body was found floating in the lower reaches of the canal. No memsahib was reported missing.

They say the guilty always return to the scene of the crime. More out of curiosity than guilt, we came together one afternoon, just before the rains broke, and crept through the shrubbery behind Miss Gamla's house.

All was silent, all was still. No one was playing in the canal. The mango trees were unattended. No one touched Miss Gamla's mangoes. Trespassers were more afraid of her than of her lathi-wielding mali.

We crept out of the bushes and advanced towards the cool, welcoming water flowing past us.

And then came a shout from the house.

'Scoundrels! Goondas! Chhokra-boys! I'll catch you this time!'

And there stood Miss Gamla, tall and menacing, alive and well, flourishing a brand-new walking stick and advancing down her steps.

'It's her ghost!' gasped Raju.

'No, she's real,' said Sushil. 'Must have got out of the canal somehow.'

'Well, at least we aren't murderers,' said Pitamber.

'No,' I agreed. 'But she'll murder us if we stand here any longer.'

Miss Gamla had been joined by her mali, the yelping peke, and a couple of other retainers.

'Let's go,' said Raju.

We fled the scene. And we never went there again. Miss Gamla had won the Battle of Panipat.

The Last Tonga Ride

It was a warm spring day in Dehradun, and the walls of the bungalow were aflame with flowering bougainvillea. The papayas were ripening. The scent of sweet peas drifted across the garden.

Grandmother sat in an easy chair in a shady corner of the veranda, her knitting needles clicking away, her head nodding now and then. She was knitting a pullover for my father. 'Delhi has cold winters,' she had said, and although the winter was still eight months away, she had set to work on getting our woollens ready.

In the Kathiawar states touched by the warm waters of the Arabian Sea, it had never been cold. But Dehra lies at the foot of the first range of the Himalayas.

Grandmother's hair was white and her eyes were not very strong, but her fingers moved quickly with the needles and the needles kept clicking all morning.

When Grandmother wasn't looking, I picked geranium leaves, crushed them between my fingers and pressed them to my nose.

I had been in Dehra with my grandmother for almost a month and I had not seen my father during this time. We had never before been separated for so long. He wrote to me every week, and sent me books and picture postcards, and I would walk to the end of the road to meet the postman as early as possible to see if there was any mail for us.

We heard the jingle of tonga bells at the gate and a familiar horse buggy came rattling up the drive.

'I'll see who's come,' I said, and ran down the veranda steps and across the garden.

It was Bansi Lal in his tonga. There were many tongas and tonga drivers in Dehra but Bansi was my favourite driver. He was young and handsome, and he always wore a clean, white shirt and pyjamas. His pony, too, was bigger and faster than the other tonga ponies.

Bansi wasn't driving a passenger, so I asked him, 'What have you come for, Bansi?'

'Your grandmother sent for me, Dost.' He did not call me 'Chota Sahib' or 'Baba', but 'Dost' and this made me feel much more important. Not every small boy could boast of a tonga driver for his friend!

'Where are you going, Granny?' I asked, after I had run back to the veranda.

'I'm going to the bank.'

'Can I come too?'

'Whatever for? What will you do in the bank?'

'Oh, I won't come inside. I'll sit in the tonga with Bansi.'

'Come along, then.'

We helped Grandmother into the back seat of the tonga, and then I joined Bansi in the driver's seat. He said something to

175

his pony and it set off at a brisk trot, out of the gate and down the road.

'Now, not too fast, Bansi,' said Grandmother, who didn't like anything that went too fast—tonga, motor car, train or bullock cart.

'Fast?' said Bansi. 'Have no fear, memsahib. This pony has never gone fast in its life. Even if a bomb went off behind us, we could go no faster. I have another pony which I use for racing when customers are in a hurry. This pony is reserved for you, memsahib.'

There was no other pony, but Grandmother did not know this, and was mollified by the assurance that she was riding in the slowest tonga in Dehra.

A ten-minute ride brought us to the bazaar. Grandmother's bank, the Allahabad Bank, stood near the Clock Tower. She was gone for about half an hour and during this period Bansi and I sauntered about in front of the shops. The pony had been left with some green stuff to munch.

'Do you have any money on you?' asked Bansi.

'Four annas,' I replied.

'Just enough for two cups of tea,' said Bansi, putting his arm round my shoulders and guiding me towards a tea stall. The money passed from my palm to his.

'You can have tea, if you like,' I offered. 'I'll have a lemonade.'

'So be it, friend. A tea and a lemonade, and be quick about it,' said Bansi to the boy in the tea shop. Presently the drinks were set before us and Bansi was making a sound rather like his pony when it drank, while I burped my way through some green, gaseous stuff that tasted more like soap than lemonade.

When Grandmother came out of the bank, she looked pensive and did not talk much during the ride back to the house except to tell me to behave myself when I leant over to pat the pony on its rump. After paying off Bansi, she marched straight indoors.

'When will you come again?' I asked Bansi.

'When my services are required, Dost. I have to make a living, you know. But I tell you what, since we are friends, the next time I am passing this way after leaving a fare, I will jingle my bells at the gate and if you are free and would like a ride—a fast ride—you can join me. It won't cost you anything. Just bring some money for a cup of tea.'

'All right—since we are friends,' I said.

'Since we are friends.'

And touching the pony very lightly with the handle of his whip, he sent the tonga rattling up the drive and out of the gate. I could hear Bansi singing as the pony cantered down the road.

Ayah was waiting for me in the bedroom, her hands resting on her broad hips—sure sign of an approaching storm.

'So you went off to the bazaar without telling me,' she began. (It wasn't enough that I had Grandmother's permission) 'And all this time I've been waiting to give you your bath.'

'It's too late now, isn't it?' I asked hopefully.

'No, it isn't. There's still an hour left for lunch. Off with your clothes!'

While I undressed, Ayah berated me for keeping the company of tonga drivers like Bansi. I think she was a little jealous.

'He is a rogue, that man. He drinks, gambles and smokes opium. He has TB and other terrible diseases. So don't you be too friendly with him, understand, Baba?'

I nodded my head sagely but said nothing. I thought Ayah was exaggerating as she always did about people, and besides, I had no intention of giving up free tonga rides.

As my father had told me, Dehra was a good place for trees, and Grandmother's house was surrounded by several kinds—peepul, neem, mango, jackfruit, papaya, and an ancient banyan tree. Some of the trees had been planted by my father and grandfather.

'How old is the jackfruit tree?' I asked Grandmother.

'Now let me see,' said Grandmother, looking very thoughtful. 'I should remember the jackfruit tree. Oh, yes, your grandfather put it down in 1927. It was during the rainy season. I remember because it was your father's birthday and we celebrated it by planting a tree—14 July 1927. Long before you were born!'

The banyan tree grew behind the house. Its spreading branches, which hung to the ground and took root again, formed a number of twisting passageways in which I liked to wander. The tree was older than the house, older than my grandparents, as old as Dehra. I could hide myself in its branches behind thick, green leaves and spy on the world below.

It was an enormous tree, about sixty feet high, and the first time I saw it I trembled with excitement because I had never seen such a marvellous tree before. I approached it slowly, even cautiously, as I wasn't sure the tree wanted my friendship. It looked as though it had many secrets. There were sounds and movements in the branches but I couldn't see who or what made the sounds.

The tree made the first move, the first overture of friendship. It allowed a leaf to fall.

The leaf brushed against my face as it floated down, but before it could reach the ground I caught and held it. I studied the leaf, running my fingers over its smooth, glossy texture. Then I put out my hand and touched the rough bark of the tree and this felt good to me. So I removed my shoes and socks as people do when they enter a holy place; and finding first a foothold and then a handhold on that broad trunk, I pulled myself up with the help of the tree's aerial roots.

As I climbed, it seemed as though someone was helping me. Invisible hands, the hands of the spirit in the tree, touched me and helped me climb.

But although the tree wanted me, there were others who were disturbed and alarmed by my arrival. A pair of parrots suddenly shot out of a hole in the trunk and with shrill cries, flew across the garden—flashes of green and red and gold. A squirrel looked out from behind a branch, saw me, and went scurrying away to inform his friends and relatives.

I climbed higher, looked up, and saw a red beak poised above my head. I shrank away, but the hornbill made no attempt to attack me. He was relaxing in his home, which was a great hole in the tree trunk. Only the bird's head and great beak were showing. He looked at me in rather a bored way, drowsily opening and shutting his eyes.

'So many creatures live here,' I said to myself. 'I hope none of them are dangerous!'

At that moment the hornbill lunged at a passing cricket. Bill and tree trunk met with a loud and resonant 'Tonk!'

I was so startled that I nearly fell out of the tree. But it was a difficult tree to fall out of! It was full of places where one could sit or even lie down. So I moved away from the hornbill, crawled along a branch which had sent out supports, and so moved quite a distance from the main body of the tree. I left its cold, dark depths for an area penetrated by shafts of sunlight.

No one could see me. I lay flat on the broad branch hidden by a screen of leaves. People passed by on the road below. A sahib in a sun helmet, his memsahib twirling a coloured silk sun umbrella. Obviously she did not want to get too brown and be mistaken for a country-born person. Behind them, a pram wheeled along by a nanny followed.

Then there were a number of Indians—some in white dhotis, some in western clothes, some in loincloths. Some with baskets on their heads. Others with coolies to carry their baskets for them. A cloud of dust, the blare of a horn, and down the road, like an out-of-condition dragon, came a Morris touring car.

Then cyclists. Then a man with a basket of papayas balanced on his head. Following him, a man with a performing monkey. This man rattled a little hand drum, and children followed man and monkey along the road. They stopped in the shade of a mango tree on the other side of the road. The little red monkey wore a frilled dress and a baby's bonnet. It danced for the children, while the man sang and played his drum.

Then came the clip-clop of a tonga pony, and Bansi's carriage could be seen rattling down the road. I called down to him and he reined in with a shout of surprise, and looked up into the branches of the banyan tree.

'What are you doing up there?' he cried.

'Hiding from my grandmother,' I answered.

'And when are you coming for that ride?'

'On Tuesday afternoon,' I said.

'Why not today?'

'Ayah won't let me. But she has Tuesdays off.'

Bansi spat red betel juice across the road. 'Your ayah is jealous,' he said.

'I know,' I replied. 'Women are always jealous, aren't they? I suppose it's because she doesn't have a tonga.'

'It's because she doesn't have a tonga driver,' said Bansi, grinning up at me. 'Never mind. I'll come on Tuesday—that's the day after tomorrow, isn't it?'

I nodded down to him, and then started backing along my branch, because I could hear Ayah calling in the distance. Bansi leant forward and smacked his pony across the rump, and the tonga shot forward.

'What were you doing up there?' asked Ayah a little later.

'I was watching a snake cross the road,' I replied. I knew she couldn't resist talking about snakes. There weren't as many in Dehra as there had been in Kathiawar and she was thrilled that I had seen one.

'Was it moving towards you or away from you?' she asked.

'It was going away.'

Ayah's face clouded over. 'That means poverty for the beholder,' she said gloomily.

Later, while scrubbing me down in the bathroom, she began to air all her prejudices, which included drunkards ('they die quickly, anyway'), misers ('they get murdered sooner or later') and tonga drivers ('they have all the vices').

'You are a very lucky boy,' she declared suddenly, peering closely at my tummy.

'Why?' I asked. 'You just said I would be poor because I saw a snake going the wrong way.'

'Well, you won't be poor for long. You have a mole on your tummy and that's very lucky. And there is one under your armpit, which means you will be famous. Do you have one on the neck? No, thank God! A mole on the neck is the sign of a murderer!'

'Do you have any moles?' I asked.

Ayah nodded seriously, and pulling her sleeve up to her shoulder, showed me a large mole high on her arm.

'What does that mean?' I wanted to know.

'It means a life of great sadness,' said Ayah gloomily.

'Can I touch it?' I asked.

'Yes, do so,' she offered, and taking my hand, she placed it against the mole.

'It's a nice mole,' I said, wanting to make Ayah happy. 'Can I kiss it?'

'You can,' answered Ayah.

I kissed her on the mole.

'That's nice,' she said.

Tuesday afternoon came at last, and as soon as Grandmother was asleep and Ayah had gone to the bazaar, I was at the gate, looking up and down the road for Bansi and his tonga. He was not long in coming. Before the tonga turned into the road,

I could hear his voice, singing to the accompaniment of the carriage bells.

He reached down, took my hand, and hoisted me on to the seat beside him. Then we went off down the road at a steady jogtrot. It was only when we reached the outskirts of the town that Bansi encouraged his pony to greater efforts. He rose in his seat, leaned forward and slapped the pony across the haunches. From a brisk trot we changed to a carefree canter. The tonga swayed from side to side. I clung to Bansi's free arm, while he grinned at me, his mouth red with betel juice.

'Where shall we go, Dost?' he asked.

'Nowhere,' I said. 'Anywhere.'

'We'll go to the river,' decided Bansi.

The 'river' was really a swift mountain stream that ran through the forests outside Dehra, joining the Ganga about fifteen miles away. It was almost dry during the winter and early summer, in flood during the monsoon.

The road out of Dehra was a gentle decline and soon we were rushing headlong through the tea gardens and eucalyptus forests, the pony's hoofs striking sparks off the metalled road, the carriage wheels groaning and creaking so loudly that I feared one of them would come off and that we would all be thrown into a ditch or into the small canal that ran beside the road. We swept through mango groves, through guava and litchi orchards, past broadleaved sal and shisham trees. Once in the sal forest, Bansi turned the tonga on to a rough cart track, and we continued along it for about a furlong, until the road dipped down to the riverbed.

'Let us go straight into the water,' said Bansi. 'You and I and the pony!' And he drove the tonga straight into the middle of the stream, where the water came up to the pony's knees.

'I am not a great one for baths,' admitted Bansi, 'but the pony needs one, and why should a horse smell sweeter than its owner?' saying which, he flung off his clothes and jumped into the water.

'Better than bathing under a tap!' he cried, slapping himself on the chest and thighs. 'Come down, Dost, and join me!'

After some hesitation I joined him, but had some difficulty in keeping on my feet in the fast current. I grabbed at the pony's tail and hung on to it, while Bansi began sloshing water over the patient animal's back.

After this, Bansi led both me and the pony out of the stream and together we gave the carriage a good washing down. I'd had a free ride and Bansi got the services of a free helper for the long overdue spring cleaning of his tonga. After we had finished the job, he presented me with a packet of *aam papar*—a sticky toffee made from mango pulp—and for some time I tore at it as a dog tears at a bit of old leather. Then I felt drowsy and lay down on the brown, sun-warmed grass. Crickets and grasshoppers were telephoning each other from tree and bush and a pair of blue jays rolled, dived and swooped acrobatically overhead.

Bansi had no watch. He looked at the sun and said, 'It is past three. When will that ayah of yours be home? She is more frightening than your grandmother!'

'She comes back at four.'

'Then we must hurry back. And don't tell her where we've been, or I'll never be able to come to your house again. Your grandmother's one of my best customers.'

'That means you'd be sorry if she died.'

'I would indeed, my friend.'

Bansi raced the tonga back to town. There was very little motor traffic in those days, and tongas and bullock carts were far more numerous than they are today.

We were back five minutes before Ayah returned. Before Bansi left, he promised to take me for another ride the following week.

The house in Dehra had to be sold. My father had not left any money; he had never realized that his health would deteriorate so rapidly from the malarial fevers which had grown in frequency. He was still planning for the future when he died. Now that my father was gone, Grandmother saw no point in staying on in India; there was nothing left in the bank and she needed money for our passages to England, so the house had to go. Dr Ghose, who had a thriving medical practice in Dehra, made her a reasonable offer, which she accepted.

Then things happened very quickly. Grandmother sold most of our belongings, because as she said, we wouldn't be able to cope with a lot of luggage. The kabaris came in droves, buying up crockery, furniture, carpets and clocks at throwaway prices. Grandmother hated parting with some of her possessions such as the carved giltwood mirror, her walnut-wood armchair and her rosewood writing desk, but it was impossible to take them with us.

They were carried away in a bullock cart.

Ayah was very unhappy at first but cheered up when Grandmother got her a job with a tea planter's family in Assam. It was arranged that she could stay with us until we left Dehra.

We went at the end of September, just as the monsoon clouds broke up, scattered, and were driven away by soft breezes from the Himalayas. There was no time to revisit the island where my father and I had planted our trees. And in the urgency and excitement of the preparations for our departure, I forgot to recover my small treasures from the hole in the banyan tree. It was only when we were already in Bansi's tonga, on the way to the station, that I remembered my top, catapult, and iron cross. Too late! To go back for them would mean missing the train.

'Hurry!' urged Grandmother nervously. 'We mustn't be late for the train, Bansi.'

Bansi flicked the reins and shouted to his pony, and for once in her life Grandmother submitted to being carried along the road at a brisk trot.

'It's five to nine,' she said, 'and the train leaves at nine.'

'Do not worry, memsahib. I have been taking you to the station for fifteen years, and you have never missed a train!'

'No,' said Grandmother. 'And I don't suppose you'll ever take me to the station again, Bansi.'

'Times are changing, memsahib. Do you know that there is now a taxi—a motor car—competing with the tongas of Dehra? You are lucky to be leaving. If you stay, you will see me starve to death!'

'We will all starve to death if we don't catch that train,' said Grandmother.

'Do not worry about the train, it never leaves on time, and no one expects it to. If it left at nine o'clock, everyone would miss it.'

Bansi was right. We arrived at the station at five minutes past nine and rushed on to the platform, only to find that the train had not yet arrived.

The platform was crowded with people waiting to catch the same train or to meet people arriving on it. Ayah was there already, standing guard over a pile of miscellaneous luggage. We sat down on our boxes and became part of the platform life at an Indian railway station.

Moving among piles of bedding and luggage were sweating, cursing coolies; vendors of magazines, sweetmeats, tea and betel leaf preparations; also stray dogs, stray people and sometimes a stray stationmaster. The cries of the vendors mixed with the general clamour of the station and the shunting of a steam engine in the yards. 'Tea, hot tea!' Sweets, papads, hot stuff, cold drinks, tooth powder, pictures of film stars, bananas, balloons, wooden toys, clay images of the gods. The platform had become a bazaar.

Ayah was giving me all sorts of warnings.

'Remember, Baba, don't lean out of the window when the train is moving. There was that American boy who lost his head last year! And don't eat rubbish at every station between here and Bombay. And see that no strangers enter the compartment. Mr Wilkins was murdered and robbed last year!'

The station bell clanged, and in the distance there appeared a big, puffing steam engine, painted green and gold and black. A stray dog with its lifetime's experience of trains, darted away across the railway lines. As the train came alongside the platform, doors opened, window shutters fell, faces appeared in the openings, and even before the train had come to a stop, people were trying to get in or out.

For a few moments there was chaos. The crowd surged backward and forward. No one could get out. No one could get in. A hundred people were leaving the train, two hundred were getting into it. No one wanted to give way.

The problem was solved by a man climbing out of a window. Others followed his example and the pressure at the doors eased as people started squeezing into their compartments.

Grandmother had taken the precaution of reserving berths in a first-class compartment, and assisted by Bansi and half a dozen coolies, we were soon inside with our entire luggage. A whistle blasted and we were off! Bansi had to jump from the running train.

As the engine gathered speed, I ignored Ayah's advice and put my head out of the window to look back at the receding platform. Ayah and Bansi were standing on the platform waving to me, and I kept waving to them until the train rushed into the darkness and the bright lights of Dehra were swallowed up in the night. New lights, dim and flickering, came into existence as we passed small villages. The stars, too, were visible and I saw a shooting star streaking through the heavens.

I remembered something that Ayah had once told me, that stars are the spirits of good men, and I wondered if that shooting star was a sign from my father that he was aware of our departure and would be with us on our journey. And I remembered something else that Ayah had said—that if one wished on a shooting star, one's wish would be granted, provided, of course, that one thrust all five fingers into the mouth at the same time!

'What on earth are you doing?' asked Grandmother staring at me as I thrust my hand into my mouth.

'Making a wish,' I answered.

'Oh,' said Grandmother.

She was preoccupied, and didn't ask me what I was wishing for; nor did I tell her.

We Rode All the Way to Delhi

In the Bicycle Age
When I was a kid
We rode all the way to Delhi,
Yes we did!
Somi and Azhar and I . . .
It took us three days
As we pressed on our pedals,
All two hundred miles
From Dehra to Delhi,
And they gave us no medals!
We sheltered in dhabas
And ate what they gave us,
But no welcoming crowd
In Delhi received us
As dusty, dishevelled
We crossed the old bridge
And rode round the city
And camped on the Ridge.

Next day we rose late—
Our bodies they ached—
So instead of cycling
All the way back again
We put our bikes on the train
And went home in style
To Dehra from Delhi,
Somi and Azhar and I . . .